NOTHING LEFT TO LOSE

TOR BOOKS BY DAN WELLS

I Am Not a Serial Killer

Mr. Monster

I Don't Want to Kill You

The Devil's Only Friend

Over Your Dead Body

Nothing Left to Lose

The Hollow City

Extreme Makeover

NOTHING LEFT TO LOSE

DAN WELLS

TOR

A TOM DOHERTY ASSOCIATES BOOK

NEW YORK

NOTHING LEFT TO LOSE

Copyright © 2017 by Dan Wells

All rights reserved.

A Tor Book
Published by Tom Doherty Associates
175 Fifth Avenue
New York, NY 10010

www.tor-forge.com

Tor® is a registered trademark of Macmillan Publishing Group, LLC.

The Library of Congress Cataloging-in-Publication Data is available upon request.

ISBN 978-0-7653-8070-8 (hardcover)
ISBN 978-0-7653-8071-5 (trade paperback)
ISBN 978-1-4668-7499-2 (ebook)

Our books may be purchased in bulk for promotional, educational, or business use. Please contact your local bookseller or the Macmillan Corporate and Premium Sales Department at 1-800-221-7945, extension 5442, or by email at MacmillanSpecialMarkets@macmillan.com.

First Edition: June 2017

Printed in the United States of America

0 9 8 7 6 5 4 3 2 1

TO JOHN. SORRY FOR PUTTING YOU
THROUGH ALL THIS. YOU DID GREAT.

ACKNOWLEDGMENTS

How can I possibly acknowledge the many quadjillions of people who contributed to this book? To this entire series? I'm frankly still kind of shocked that the first one got published, let alone six of them in a bunch of different formats and countries and languages. So let's start at the beginning:

Thank you to my parents, who raised me as a reader. Thank you to my teachers: Mrs. Richardson, who helped me become a storyteller; Mrs. Coen, who taught me to love words; to Mrs. Hooper, who assigned us to read Dragonsong in sixth grade and showed me that fun books were every bit as good as important ones. And thank you to whoever wrote that news article I was too young to read about a guy who kidnapped little boys, took their pictures, and killed them with a hammer. Horror is everywhere, but realizing it was right in my own backyard changed the way I look at pretty much everything.

Thank you to Dave Wolverton, Linda Adams, and Marion "Doc" Smith. Thank you to my first writing group: Ben Olsen, Nate Goodrich, and Brandon Sanderson. Thank you to the staff of The Leading Edge, both during my time there and all the time before and since. Thank you to Michelle Ward and Jonathan Maberry, who helped me find my agent, and thank you to my wonderful agent, Sara Crowe, who is the best and greatest agent in the world. Thank you to Moshe Feder, who took a chance on some doofus with a horror story and gave me my first professional sale. You're awesome. Thank you to Carsten Polzin, my editor in Germany, who paid me enough to actually do this full time, and who showed me how to appeal to a broader audience. Thank you to Alexis Saarela and Patty Garcia and Paul Stevens and Tom Doherty and Kathleen Doherty and Amy Stapp and Theresa Nielsen Hayden and Irene Gallo and a massive army of other amazing people at Tor who do such phenomenal work behind the scenes. And a huge thank you to my editor, Whitney Ross. You're the best.

Thank you to Brandon Sanderson (again), Mary Robinette Kowal, Howard Tayler, Jordan Sanderson, and everyone who's ever been on, talked about, or listened to *Writing Excuses*. Thank you to my writing groups and readers, including but not limited to Alan Layton, Kaylynn Zobell, Ethan Skarstedt, Sandra Tayler, Eric James Stone, Janci Patterson, Drew Olds, Emily Sanderson, Steve Diamond, Maija-Liisa Phipps, Ethan Sproat, and many more. Thank you to the concoms and booksellers and other authors who've promoted my work, and given me the opportunity and advice on how to do it; I'll give an extra special shout-out here to Kevin J. Anderson and Jude Feldman and Alan

Beatts. And thank you to my assistants, Chersti Nieveen and Kenna Blaylock.

Thank you to Elmore Leonard, A. A. Milne, and Ke$ha. I don't have to explain myself to you.

Thank you to Billy O'Brien, Robbie Ryan, Nick Ryan, James Harris, Max Records, Christopher Lloyd, Laura Fraser, Toby Froud, Todd Jones, and a massive cast and crew too numerous to name. You made our movie amazing, and I will love it forever.

I sought my death and found it in my womb,
I lookt for life and saw it was a shade,
I trode the earth and knew it was my tomb,
And now I die, and now I am but made.
The glass is full, and now the glass is run,
And now I live, and now my life is done.

—CHIDIOCK TICHBORNE, "ELEGY"

CHAPTER 1

There are only so many ways to get a good look at a dead body.

You can always just make your own, of course, which is what most people do. It's quick, it's cheap, and you can do it with things you have lying around your own home: a hammer, a kitchen knife, a relative who won't shut up, and bam. Your very own corpse. As DIY projects go, murder is easier and more common than painting your living room, though—to be fair—significantly harder to hide. And it has other downsides as well: first, it's murder. So there's that. Second, and more pertinent to my own situation, it's only really helpful if the dead body you want to see is one you have ready access to while it's still alive. With the really good bodies, this is rarely the case. Let's say you want to examine a specific corpse, like, oh, I don't know, an old lady who died of mysterious causes in a small town in Arizona. Just to pull an example out of the air. Then it gets much harder.

If you need to look at a specific body, it helps to be an actual cop or, better yet, an agent of the FBI. You could mock up some quick excuse as to why this particular dead body was a key part of your investigation, go in, flash a badge, done. It might even be true, which would be a nice side benefit but isn't really necessary. If you weren't actually in law enforcement but you knew enough about it, you could waltz in with a fake badge and try to accomplish the same thing. But if you were also, for example, eighteen years old, convincing the local law enforcement to believe you would be easier said than done. The same goes for a teenager pretending to be a coroner, pretending to be a forensic examiner, and pretending to be a reporter. I've used the "I'm researching something for the school paper" line a couple of times, and it works well enough, but only when the something you're researching isn't a decaying human being.

That leaves three main options: first, if you can get there quick enough, you can try to trick the coroner into believing that you're the new driver for the local mortuary, assigned to pick up the body and deliver it to the embalmer. You'd need some fake paperwork but, honestly, not as much as you might think. And since "driver" is an entry-level position, your age isn't going to matter. And if you grew up in a mortuary and assisted in the family business since you were ten and knew the whole industry backward and forward—again, just to pull an example out of the air—you could do it pretty easily. But only if you got there in time.

Let's say you didn't, because you were two states away and travel solely by hitchhiking (or, honestly, whatever reason—you just can't get there in time, is the important part). In that case, you move on to the second option, which requires more or less the same skills: break in to the mortuary after hours and show yourself around. I say "more or less the same skills" because you never know how good the mortuary's security system is going to be, and you're a teenage mortician, not a cat burglar. In a small town, or even a biggish city, if the funeral home is old enough, you might be able to make it work because they don't always have the funds to update their equipment. It's kind of an industry problem.

But let's say they did update their equipment—no cameras, but an alarm with a motion sensor—and that you definitely don't want to get caught breaking into a funeral home. I mean, I guess nobody would want to get caught breaking into anything, but let's say for this example that you really, really don't want it. Let's even go so far as to say that the law enforcement agencies we mentioned earlier, which our totally hypothetical teenage mortuary expert was briefly tempted to impersonate, are, in fact, actively searching for him. So anything illegal is out of the question. That leaves us with only one option: we have to wait until the mortuary opens its doors, pulls the corpse out of the back room, and invites anyone who wants to see it to just come in and look at it. Which is never going to happen, right?

Wrong. It's called a viewing, and it happens every day. They don't let you really get in there and poke around, but it's better than nothing. And Kathy Schrenk, a little old lady who died under mysterious circumstances in the Arizona town of Lewisville, had a viewing today. And a teenage mortician with an FBI background stood outside hoping his suit didn't look too filthy.

Hi. My name is John Cleaver, and my life sounds kind of weird when I describe it like this.

I'll describe it another way, but it's not going to sound any more normal: I hunt monsters. I used to do it alone, and then for a while I did it with a team of government specialists, and then the monsters found us and killed almost everyone, and now I hunt them alone again. The monsters are called Withered, or sometimes Cursed, or sometimes Blessed if you catch one in a good mood, but that's pretty rare these days. They're old, and tired, and clinging to life more out of stubbornness than anything else. They used to be human, but they gave up some intrinsic part of themselves—their memory, or their emotions, or their identity; it's different for each of them—and now they aren't human anymore. One of them told me that they were more than human, and less, all at the same time. They've spent ten thousand years with incredible powers, ruling the world as kings and gods, but now they just grit their teeth and survive.

The mysterious nature of Kathy Schrenk's death is classic tabloid news: she drowned far away from water, her body soaked while everything around her was dry as a bone. Weird, but not automatically supernatural; Miss Marple could probably knock this one out on her lunch break. Nine times out of ten—nine thousand times out of nine thousand and one—it's just a plain old human— jealous, or angry, or greedy, or bored. We're horrible people, when it comes right down to it. Hardly worth saving at all.

But what else am I going to do? Stop?

I stared at the mortuary a little longer: Ottessen Brothers Funeral Home. I picked a piece of lint off my sleeve. Smoothed my hair. Picked another piece of lint. It was now or never.

This is what I'd been doing for months now, ever since the team had died and I'd sent Brooke home and I'd gone out on my own, hunting the Withered with no backup and no guides and no intel. I looked for anomalies, and I followed them up. Most of them didn't pan out, and I simply moved on.

I went inside.

My hypothetical situation from earlier, about growing

up in a mortuary, wasn't hypothetical. You probably guessed that. My parents were both morticians, and we lived in a little apartment upstairs from the chapel. I started helping with funerals when I was ten, and with the actual embalming a few years later. Stepping into Ottessen Brothers was like stepping into my past. The tastefully understated decorations, at least a decade behind the times; the little half-moon table with a signing book and a faux-fancy pen. The unsettled mix of sophistication and generic religion, and a drinking fountain by the wall. I touched the wallpaper—elegant but rugged, designed to withstand bustling crowds and untrained pallbearers—and thought about my home. I hadn't seen it in almost three years, though I'd glimpsed it now and then on the news. My sister and my aunt ran the mortuary now, but who knew how long that was going to last. They couldn't run it on their own. My father wouldn't help, and my mother . . . well, she wasn't around to help either, was she?

Her corpse had been so damaged that I couldn't embalm her. It was the one thing we'd shared, and even that was taken away.

The crowd in the Schrenk viewing was sparse, mostly other old ladies not long from a viewing of their own. A handful of old men. Someone had placed a table by the door with an arrangement of photos and memorabilia, and while there were plenty of group shots, Schrenk was all alone in the portraits. Never married, never had kids. Some photos included what looked like her twin sister.

One of the photos showed Schrenk standing in front of the mortuary itself, her arm around a thick-waisted woman somewhere in her fifties. An odd place for a photo—maybe another friend's funeral? But no, neither of them wore go-to-a-funeral kind of clothes. Employees, then? The rest of the table was covered with various little yarn hats and scarves, so I assumed Schrenk was a knitter.

I moved past the table and into the viewing room itself: the coffin on the far wall, flanked by flags, with various chairs and sofas scattered around the edges of the room, most of them full of old women having hushed conversations. One corner held a refreshments table with an assortment of crumbly cookies.

"I think she looks terrible," said an old lady by the food, "whispering" to a small cluster of concerned women. I couldn't tell if she was pretending to whisper but wanted to be heard, or if she legitimately didn't know how to regulate her own volume. "I've never seen a body look less lifelike in my life."

I walked slowly past them toward the coffin, trying to look like I belonged.

"Hello," said a man, stepping forward and offering his hand. I shook it. "Are you a friend of Kathy's?" He looked about sixty, maybe sixty-five.

"Acquaintance," I said quickly, spooling out my pre-packaged lie. "She was friends with my grandmother, but she couldn't make it today so she wanted me to pay our respects."

"Wonderful!" he said. "What was your grandmother's name?"

"Julia." I didn't know any Julias, but it was as good a name as any.

"I think I heard Kathy mention her," said the man, though I couldn't tell if I'd stumbled onto an accidentally accurate name or if he was just being polite. "And what was your name, young man?"

"Robert," I said, hoping it was generic enough that he would forget it if anyone asked. I tried to never use the same name twice, thanks to the whole FBI thing. I looked at him a moment: a well-worn suit, too high on the ankles; a plain white shirt already fraying at the creases in the cuffs and collar. This was a man who wore these clothes a lot, and I made an educated guess: "Do you work for the mortuary?"

"I do," he said, and offered his hand again. "Harold Ottessen, I'm the driver."

"The driver?" There goes my bit about drivers being young. "I assume your brother is the mortician, then?"

"He was," said Harold. "But I'm afraid he passed away about twenty years ago."

"I'm sorry to hear that."

"These things happen," he said. "We'd know, in our family. Margo runs things now; she's around here somewhere."

I nodded, already bored of the small talk. "It was very nice to meet you, Harold. I'm going to pay my respects."

He nodded and offered his hand to shake a third time, but before I could extricate myself, another old lady walked up with a stern look.

"It's completely disgraceful," she said. "Can't you do anything about it?"

"I've told you," said Harold, "this is just how they look sometimes."

"But it's your job," said the woman. "Why are we even here if you can't do your job?"

I was desperate to see the body by now, wondering what kind of horror everyone was complaining about, so I left Harold to fend for himself and walked to the coffin. There was another woman standing beside it, though she was much younger—barely older than me, maybe nineteen or twenty, and dark-skinned. Mexican, maybe? She screwed her face into an unhappy scowl but hid it when she saw me out of the corner of her eye.

The body was, after all the anxious hype, pretty normal. Kathy had been thin in her photos and looked thin now, with curly gray hair and a pale, gaunt face. I'd been expecting some visible injuries, something I could tie directly to a Withered attack—maybe a giant bite taken out of her face. Or, failing that, some kind of problem with the embalming itself, like maybe they'd set the features poorly and now she had sunken eyelids or hollow cheeks or something. Something to justify the mortified attitude from all of her friends. What I saw was far simpler, and so surprising I said it out loud.

"They did her makeup wrong."

"Excuse me?" asked the girl next to me.

"Sorry," I said. "It just took me by surprise, is all."

"You're a dick," she said.

"Excuse me?"

She smirked. "It just took me by surprise, is all. Isn't that what we're doing, narrating our lives out loud? Let me keep going: We're standing by my dead friend. Some random douchebag is mocking her makeup, of all things."

"I'm sorry," I said, "I'll shut up now."

"Oh good, we're still doing it. I'll stop talking, too, and then I'll stand here waiting for you to leave."

This was going great. "Just . . . give me a minute." I tried to ignore the young woman and looked at the body again. Part of a mortician's job—arguably half of it, after the actual embalming—was to make the dead person's body look as close as possible to what it looked like when they were alive. Poor Ms. Schrenk looked wrong, in ways a person off the street probably couldn't put a finger on but which all worked together to make her seem *off*. Profoundly corpselike, instead of resting in peace. It was disconcerting, but a trained eye could see that they'd actually only missed a couple of key things.

First of all, the foundation looked good. Dead bodies don't have blood in their skin, so they look much lighter than they did in life, but the mortuary's makeup artist had used a dark foundation under a lighter one to add some color back into her face. The other major problem was the eyes, which tended to have dark circles around them, like black-eye bruises. But the makeup artist had hidden those as well. And that was hard to do right, which is why it was so confusing that whoever had done Kathy Schrenk's makeup had missed a much simpler detail: shading. We're so used to seeing people vertical, that when we see them lying flat, especially in the weird light of a viewing room, their facial features look all wrong. They don't have the right shading, in subtle places like the nostrils and the lips. A trained mortuary makeup artist should have caught that, but nobody had.

The woman next to me spoke again. "Are you from Cottwell's?"

"Cottwell's?"

"Yes, genius, Cottwell's. 'Lewisville's oldest funeral home,' or whatever garbage tagline they're using these days. You're not a spy or anything?"

"I'm not from Lewisville," I said. "But I am from a mortuary, kind of. I apologize again for being rude about your friend." I paused then, thinking for a moment. Why would she be so bothered by Cottwell's, or think they were sending a spy? I could only think of one reason. "Do you work here, at this mortuary?"

She narrowed her eyes. "How do you know that if you're not a spy?"

"Why would one mortuary spy on another one?"

"I don't know, what did they tell you when they hired you?"

"They didn't. . . . Look, I'm sorry I was rude, okay? I insulted your friend who passed away, and I also apparently insulted your friend who works as the makeup artist—oh crap."

She flashed a smug smile, watching the realization hit me. "Yup."

"It's you, isn't it? You're the makeup artist."

"*Fill-in* makeup artist," she said. "Normally I'm just an embalmer. It's kind of funny to watch how slowly you figure all this out."

"I bet it is," I said. I needed more information and this woman was my only lead so far, so antagonistic or not, I tried to draw out the conversation. "So, who's the permanent makeup artist?"

"Don't worry; you'll get this one too."

I closed my eyes as yet another piece of the puzzle fell into place. "It's Kathy Schrenk."

"Amazing."

"That's why a twenty-year-old is friends with an old lady," I said. "You're coworkers. And that's why the makeup is wrong, because the only person who knows how to do it is dead, and none of you wanted to ask the Cottwell's makeup person for help."

"Does that make us sound petty?" she asked. "Because I want to make sure we sound petty."

"I'm not a spy from a rival mortuary," I said, "as thrilling as that BBC miniseries would be." I looked around the room quickly—no one was looking at the body but us. "But I am a mortician, and I can help you fix this." I looked at the young woman again. She had bronze skin—not super dark, but dark enough. "Do you have some makeup handy?"

She raised her eyebrow. "You want to mess with her makeup right here?"

"It'll take me sixty seconds at the most," I said. "Close your eyes."

"Hell no."

"I'm not going to hurt anything," I said. "The problem is the shading—like here, and here. You did a pretty good job on her, but the shading thing is unique to dead bodies, which is why you didn't think to do it. It's super simple, but I need some dark brown makeup, and I'm guessing that your eye shadow will be perfect. May I please look at it?"

She stared at me, probably trying to decide if I was crazy, then sighed and closed her eyes lightly, so the eyelid rested over the eyeball without wrinkling. I studied it a moment, then looked back at the dead body.

"Yeah, that should be perfect," I said. "Do you have it on you? I can fix this in sixty seconds, tops."

She dug in her purse and pulled out a small makeup compact, but when I reached for it she pulled it back slightly, tightening her grip. She glanced around the room, seeing Harold still locked in conversation with a crowd of displeased future customers. The girl sighed and looked back at me. "Sixty seconds?"

"At the most."

"And I get to stab you if you screw it up?"

"With the pointy implement of your choice," I said. She hesitated another moment, and then surrendered the eye shadow. I opened it up. The color looked good. I picked up the sponge, brushed it over the makeup, then dabbed a little on my arm to gauge how easily it transferred from brush to skin. I didn't want to smear a huge blob on the dead woman's face. It went onto my arm fairly smoothly, so I started dabbing small, subtle lines on the body's face—lightly at first, then more confidently as the old muscle memory took over. The crevices around the nostrils; the philtrum above the upper lip; the line below the lower lip; a dot or two on the chin. I paused partway through, breathing deeply, savoring the unexpected intensity of my emotions as I worked—it was shocking, almost embarrassing, how *right* it felt to be working on a dead body again. This is who I'd been for years, and who I'd always hoped to be for the rest of my life. A mortician. I felt a reverence for death, and for the caretakers who guided the bodies of the dead into their final repose, so to be here again, in this place, touching this body, was . . .

I realized that a tear had tracked down my face and I wiped it quickly, hoping the girl hadn't seen it. I looked at the body one last time, moving my head to see it from different angles, and dabbed one last bit of makeup on the chin. I clapped the box closed and handed it back to the girl. But before she could take it, Kathy Schrenk's twin sister inserted herself between us, leveling her finger at the body in a sign of accusation and said:

"See! Look how . . . oh."

"Let me see," said another woman, her voice stronger than the others, and I turned to see a whole group walking up behind me: Harold; a gaggle of old, frail women; and the large woman I'd seen earlier in Kathy's photo. Margo, I assumed. The funeral director. She stepped forward, looked at the body, then looked back at the women.

"She looks fine to me."

"Are you blind?" asked one of the old ladies. "She looks like you dredged her out of a river."

Margo stepped aside, allowing more of the old women to approach, and one by one their eyes softened as they looked at their friend.

"She looks wonderful," said one.

"So peaceful," said another.

"It must have been our eyes," said the sister. "Or the light." She looked at Margo and smiled. "We're so sorry to have bothered you. I think maybe one of these lights was malfunctioning before, but she looks wonderful now."

"Thank you," said Margo. "And thank you for coming."

As the women crowded around the casket, Harold looked up, confused, and Margo pulled the Mexican girl aside. "That's not what she looked like when we wheeled her out of the back," Margo whispered. "What'd you do?"

"Calculated risk," said the girl, and pointed at me. "If I can't trust some rando off the street, who *can* I trust?"

Margo glanced at me, sizing me up, then looked back at the girl and raised her eyebrows. "You let someone touch a body? Without consulting me?"

"It worked," said the girl. "You saw what a good job he did."

Margo sighed, then looked at me again, raising her chin in a way that made her look abruptly open and professional. "Thank you very much for your help." She stuck out her hand. "I'm Margo Bennett."

"Robert," I said, and shook her hand.

"Where'd you train?"

"Family mortuary," I said. "No formal training."

"You do good work," she said, and turned back to the girl. "Next time, ask me first."

"I will."

Margo nodded and left, and the girl looked at me again. "Well then. I guess I don't get to stab you."

"It's not as fun as people expect," I said, handing back her compact. I wasn't much for small talk, or really any talk for that matter, but I still needed information, and this was probably my best chance to get it. "What did you say your name was?"

"Jasmyn," she said. "With a *Y*."

"Nice to meet you, Jasmyn." I almost said "Jasmyn with a *Y*," but small talk or not, I still had some self-respect. "So you're, um, training as an embalmer?"

"I am," she said. "About a year now."

I nodded, and then wondered if I was nodding too much, and stopped. I had the opportunity to ask questions, but I didn't know which questions to ask. "So." I hesitated way too long, trying to think of a follow-up. "How do you like it?"

"You're definitely not a spy."

"Why not?"

"Because you suck at it. This is seriously, like, the worst small talk I have ever heard."

"To be fair, I hate talking to people." It was a risk, but if I was reading her right she'd respond to it.

She smirked and rolled her eyes. "Yeah, tell me about it. People are the worst."

Bingo.

"I'm going to drown my sorrows in cookies," I said, and pointed to the side table. "Want one?"

"They're also the worst," she said. "But why not?"

We walked to the food table and I picked up a cookie. It fell in half partway to my mouth, the bottom falling back onto the tray.

"See?" said Jasmyn. She took a crumbly bite. "Margo insists on them, but she won't pay for good ones."

"Our mortuary never had cookies," I said.

"That's exactly what I tell her," she said. "Nobody has cookies at a viewing, unless the family brings them or something." She took another bite. "Maybe she has stock in the cookie company."

"Does Cottwell's do cookies?" I asked.

Jasmyn shook her head. "No. So maybe that's why Margo does—she's trying to stand out."

"So, um . . ." I wanted to ask about the body, and I thought I'd finally come up with a normal way to do it. Well, normal-ish. "So Kathy Schrenk drowned, right?"

"So they say," said Jasmyn. "Nobody knows how, though. She was in her backyard, and she doesn't have a pool or anything. And she doesn't live anywhere near the canal."

This was where I relied on her inexperience as an embalmer. "Drowned bodies are so weird," I said. "You always get that weird black goop." This, of course, was a lie, and a fairly transparent one. Nobody who drowns has black goop, unless they literally drown in a pool of black goop. I mean, the goop wouldn't have come from the drowning, it would have come from a Withered. They called it soulstuff, and it was like a kind of greasy ash that got left behind at a lot of their attacks. I think it's what their bodies were made of, under their human-looking disguise, because every time I killed one they dissolved into a noxious little pile of it. If Schrenk was killed by a Withered, Jasmyn might have seen some soulstuff during the embalming. And if not, well, she was new enough at her job that she wouldn't necessarily call me on the lie.

I looked back at Jasmyn, feeling a surge of hope—could this be it?

Nope. She looked confused. "Really?" she asked. "Black goop?"

I sighed. "Sometimes," I said. "I figured it didn't hurt to ask."

"Hey Jazz," said Harold, "can you help me with something?"

"Sure," said Jasmyn, and she hurried after him. I retreated to the wall, wondering what to do next but mostly just happy to be in a mortuary again—not because it was especially wonderful, but because it was familiar. The people and the wall hangings and the music and the casket and the body. I didn't really know how to hunt monsters, though I'd been doing it for years. I didn't really know how to hitchhike and be on the road and evade the police and how to do all the things my life had forced me to do. But I knew how to be in a mortuary. I was never more comfortable anywhere else than there.

A movement caught my eye, and I looked across the room to see another woman had just come in through the doors. She looked about thirty, but she wore an old-style, A-line dress, so filthy it looked like she'd been wearing it for years. Her hair hung in ratty tendrils around her face. The other guests shied away from her as she stepped in, looked around, and then focused on me. I glanced around for the mortuary staff—for Jasmyn, or Harold, or Margo—but they'd all stepped out for something. The ragged woman walked toward me, and I could see that her face and arms were as dirty as her clothes; her nails were chipped and crusted with old blood; and her feet were bare and streaked with grime. She walked strangely, like she was unaccustomed to it, and kept her eyes locked on my face. She stopped a few feet in front of me, staring.

"I know you," she said at last.

"I don't think so," I said.

"Do you know me?"

I shook my head. "I don't. I'm sorry."

The woman stared again, then leaned in close.

"Run from Rain," she whispered.

Then she turned around and ran out the door.

CHAPTER 2

Run from Rain.

It was one of the last things Brooke had told me, one of the last leads she'd dug up from the recesses of her memory. Ten thousand years of dead girls and a supernatural killer, and all of them were terrified of "Rain," though we'd never figured out who or what Rain was. Another Withered, we'd assumed. Maybe one of the last ones left.

And now, after months of searching, I'd found another piece of the puzzle.

I ran outside, looking for the dazed, dirty woman who'd said the words, but she was gone. Homeless, maybe? Unbalanced, almost certainly. Or maybe it was something more sinister—was she a victim of Rain, somehow? Someone who'd been enslaved to a paranormal monster, or who'd been attacked and managed to escape, or maybe just someone who'd seen an attack and been broken by the thought of it. Withered attacks could be horrifying, mind-shattering things, upending everything you thought you knew about the world and the way it functioned.

Or maybe she'd survived a different kind of Withered attack—not by Rain, but by Nobody. Nobody killed by possessing young girls and using their own bodies to commit suicide; Brooke had lived through it, but she'd gained an untold horde of Withered memories as a result. That's how she could remember things like "Run from Rain." Now here was another girl with the same dark memory and the same broken, disorganized mind and . . . in ten thousand years, Brooke can't have been the only person to survive an attack from Nobody, could she? Maybe this lost girl was another.

Whoever the girl was, at least one connection seemed obvious: a Withered named Rain, in a city where someone had drowned without water. It couldn't be a coincidence. I had to stay in Lewisville and I had to learn everything I could about this killer, starting with the body of Kathy Schrenk.

And the best way to do that was to wait.

There was a bus stop nearby, on the heat-blasted side of the cracked asphalt road, and I sat there in the sun and waited. My backpack containing all my worldly possessions was back in the bus station where I'd showered after hitchhiking into town; storing it had cost me a dollar, which probably meant that I couldn't eat dinner that night, but it was better than bringing the whole dusty thing with me to the mortuary. Nothing said "ignore and/or suspect this person" like showing up in a clean, well-kept place with an old, dirty backpack bursting with clothes. That marked you as a drifter, and I needed these people to trust me. Now more than ever.

The viewing had started at four in the afternoon, was scheduled to last until six. After a funeral the morticians would be off to the cemetery and out in the hearse and running all over for another few hours at least, but after a viewing they simply wheeled the casket back into the fridge and locked up for the night. I waited at the bus stop, waving each bus past as they trundled by my bench, and watching as the people moved in and out of the funeral home, paying their respects, sharing their gossip, eating their crumbly cookies, and going away. At 6:10 the last few mourners hobbled out to their cars—a sixty-year-old son holding the door for his eighty-year-old mother—and I stood up and walked back into the building. The AC was an arctic storm after so much time in the Arizona sun, and I shivered as I stood in the doorway and looked for the workers. Harold was closing the viewing room door, kicking a doorstop out of the way with his foot, when he looked up and saw me.

"Viewing's just closed, I'm afraid—" and then he

stopped, squinted, and recognized me. "You were in here earlier. Forget something?"

"I was wondering if I could speak to Margo," I said. Harold may have been an Ottessen Brother, but it was clear who made the decisions around the mortuary.

Harold closed the door and tested the handle, then turned back toward me. "What's this pertaining to?"

"I'd like to apply for the job."

"Job?"

"The makeup tech," I said, gesturing toward the door. "Your last one died, and none of the rest of you know the work." I shrugged. "I do."

Harold stared at me a moment, then bobbed his head up and down and up and down, like a chicken. "Okay," he said. "I guess that's true enough. I won't be able to hire you myself, though. You'll have to talk to Margo."

I hid the confused frown that tried to creep over my face: why would he say that when I'd asked for Margo in the first place? Maybe he was bitter about his lost authority. He didn't seem bitter, though. Just . . . lost.

"Come with me," he said at last, and I followed him down the hall toward an office. Harold was tall and lanky in a way that looked like he'd probably been skinny in his youth, though now he was sagging and hunched, like his body was old glass slowly flowing to the bottom of a pane. He opened the office door without knocking, and I waited in the hall while he stepped inside. Margo was sitting behind a broad, wooden desk that was covered with papers, a monitor, and keyboard—not the fancy desk where she held meetings with the families of the deceased, but the real desk where actual work got done. Jasmyn was sitting across from her, looking more than a little downcast, and I couldn't help but wonder if she was getting chastised for my brazen, midviewing corpse makeover.

"Excuse me, Margo," said Harold. "But that boy's here to see you."

She didn't ask which boy, she simply looked past him to the hall and studied me, like a buyer in a museum. The only other morticians I'd ever really known had been my parents, and neither had held anything like this woman's quiet authority. My mother had been a bundle of nerves, always stumbling on the edge of fearing she'd done too much or not enough; my father had been loud and gregarious, earning trust not through his presence but through his voice, in a never-ending stream of patter and charm. Margo didn't talk or scurry or try, she simply *was*. It was easy to see, just from standing in the hallway and being looked at, why Harold so easily left the running of the business to her.

"Why don't you two give Robert and I the room," she said at last, and without argument, Jasmyn and Harold walked out, and I walked in. "Go ahead and close that door," said Margo, so I did, and the whole situation felt so subservient I couldn't help but chafe against it. I scanned the room in a second, identified the chair that would be most awkward for her to look at, and sat down without waiting for an invitation. In Margo's presence, it felt like an act of brazen rebellion.

Margo looked at me, silent for a moment, then swiveled her chair toward me and leaned back heavily. "You did a good job on Kathy," she said. "She was a good friend of mine, and I thank you for that."

"You're welcome," I said. "Thank you for the opportunity. It's kind of been a while."

Margo nodded. "Family business, you told me earlier?"

"I did indeed."

"There's a lot of that in this industry," said Margo, and she leaned forward to shuffle some papers around her desk. "Something about the spiritual nature of it, I suspect. If your daddy's an accountant or a plumber you might still grow up to be anything else, but when your daddy's a mortician, you grow up to be a mortician."

"Is that how you got into it?" I asked. "One of the Ottessen sisters?"

"The Ottessen daughter-in-law," said Margo. "So I suppose I married into it, but it's become my life just as much as anyone else's. That's why I'm still here going on twenty years after Jonathan's passing."

"Did you get to embalm him?" I asked. I don't know why I asked, it just came out. Sometimes small talk reveals a lot more about you than you want it to.

Margo stopped moving papers and looked up. "Nobody lets me do anything," she said. "I do what I please." She considered me for a moment before looking back at her papers, sliding a series of yellow forms into a neat stack. "Who did you not get to embalm? Your father?"

"Neither one," I said, though the topic made me uncomfortable. I didn't like talking about my family much, now that they were mostly gone. "My father's still alive, though, as far as I know, so I suppose there's always hope."

"Small-town mortuary," said Margo. She slid the yellow stack into a worn brown folder, then pulled another folder from a drawer behind her desk. "Embalming all your neighbors and your friends' grandparents. People you know. And then your parents go away, and you don't have anything left, so you start, what, walking the Earth? Thumbing rides through back roads and farmland?"

I cocked my head to the side, looking at her. How had she guessed so much? And what was she thinking about it? Was she accusing me or deciphering me?

"Ma'am, I'd like to ask for a job."

Margo sighed and tapped her folder on the desk. "I know. And I'm trying to figure out what kind of a young man would show up at a funeral home for someone he doesn't know and then expect a job out of it."

I froze. How had she guessed that so easily?

"I saw you sitting at the bus stop for an hour and a half," said Margo, as if she were reading my mind, "waving past all four buses that stopped to pick you up." She handed me the folder. "I saw the way you looked in that viewing room, all lost and come home at the same time. And I guess you could say I saw the way Jasmyn showed up here last year, just as lost and looking for someplace to stay and something to do. I never had any children of my own, but I know a wayward duckling when I see one."

I opened the folder to find a job application inside, printed with *Ottessen Brothers Funeral Home* in bold letters at the top. I scanned the page quickly, looking at all the empty fields it wanted me to fill in: name, birthplace, social security number, current address and phone number. I closed the folder, but I didn't give it back.

"I can't give you most of this information."

"Drifters rarely can."

"I'd . . . very much like this job, though."

"Just put down what you can, and we'll fill in the rest as time goes by."

"As time goes by." So this wasn't a job application; this sounded like she was hiring me outright, and I was just providing data for her records. I opened the folder again, took a pen from the desk, and wrote *Robert* at the top of the page. I hadn't thought of a last name yet, so I hesitated just a moment before writing down the first fake one I could think of: *Jensen.* Marci's last name. I stared at the form for a minute, then handed it to Margo.

She raised her eyebrow in surprise. "Just a name and that's it?"

"We can fill in the rest as time goes by."

She stared at me a moment, then shrugged and took the folder. "The things I do for wayward ducklings. You have a place to stay?"

"I do not."

"You can have Jasmyn's old room—she lived in the spare room off the side until about five, six weeks ago when she got her own place. 'Asserting her independence.' I'll expect you to do the same sooner or later."

"If you tell me to do it, how independent can it really be?"

She stared at me again, then a slow smile crept across her face. "I think I'm going to like you, Robert. You don't happen to be good with books, too?"

"Like, reading?"

"Like adding," she said, and tapped a ledger on the corner of the desk. "Accounting. Our books are sloppy, and we need someone to clean them up, make sure everything's square."

"I'm definitely not the guy for that."

"That's fine, I guess. I've got a friend who can do it. Hoping I wouldn't have to pay his rates, though." She sighed. "Let me go find Harold, see if we can get your room squared away." She heaved herself to her feet, and I pointed quickly toward the computer on the side of the desk.

"Do you mind if I use that real quick? I need to look something up online."

"No porn," she said, and opened the door. "Password is Norman's last name."

She stayed there, watching me, and I realized that the password was a final test: if I was really the mortician's son

I said I was, I'd know exactly which Norman she was talking about, and what his last name was. I walked around to the keyboard, shook the mouse to wake it up, and typed *Greenbaum*. Norman Greenbaum's "Spirit in the Sky" was the most requested song at funerals in America, and most morticians knew it by heart. The login screen disappeared and the desktop opened, and Margo smiled. She turned and walked away down the hall. I opened the browser.

I'd originally read about Kathy Schrenk's mysterious death on a Reddit thread for weird news, and I wanted to see if they'd added more information. It turned out Margo had blocked Reddit on her machine, though, so I did a general web search for "Kathy Schrenk Lewisville" and got a few hits. A few new articles but no new info. I searched "Run From Rain," but I'd searched that a thousand times already and there was never anything useful. I searched a few more strings that I thought might lead to more info about the drowning but nothing turned up. I stared at the computer for a full minute before finally typing in a new search:

"Brooke Watson."

The first two results were for Facebook pages of women I'd never met, but the third was a news article about my friend and her family moving away from Clayton County. An undisclosed location, in protective custody after her "kidnapping." I couldn't really argue with the term. She'd insisted on coming with me after the others were killed, and she'd cried and screamed when I'd finally brought her back, saying she never wanted to leave me, but . . . Well, I don't want to say that she wasn't fit to make her own decisions, but it's hard to argue that she was. The article said she was going into a new therapy facility, and I hoped it worked. She'd been through too much, and mostly because of me.

I was about to click off the page when a little blue word at the bottom caught my eye: my own name, John Cleaver. I clicked the link and found a related story about my sister, begging me to come home. There was even a video, but I didn't watch it; the transcript was enough. "Lauren Cleaver released an official statement today asking her brother John, a wanted fugitive, to turn himself in. 'Please John, we love you. We miss you. We're so thrilled and grateful that you brought Brooke home, but please, we want you back too.'" I didn't read the rest. I closed the page, cleared the browser history, and stood up just as Margo and Jasmyn came bustling back into the room.

"Out of the way, Robert," said Margo, barely pausing before barreling past me to the desk. I moved to the corner, out of the way, and Margo plopped down heavily while Jasmyn started rifling through a filing cabinet on the far wall. "Do you have those forms?"

"Right here," said Jasmyn. She flipped through a few more files while Margo clicked anxiously on the computer screen.

"What happened?" I asked.

"You're getting your baptism by fire," said Margo,

though she and Jasmyn immediately cringed. "Dammit, I didn't mean to say it that way."

"Here," said Jasmyn, pulling two different-colored forms out of the cabinet. "Regular and cremation."

Aha. "We're going to cremate somebody?"

"If we do we'll be finishing what somebody already started," said Margo. "Just got a call from Cecily, my girl down at the coroner's office. They've got a body burnt half to a crisp; figure we'll be getting it by this weekend." She stopped her clicking and looked up at me. "If the family wants an open casket, have you done makeup on third-degree burns before?"

"Once," I said. In truth I'd only seen it done, as my mom and Margaret worked on a boy who'd been trapped in a house fire. I'd read a lot about it, though, and I figured I knew enough to make it work. All-consuming obsessions have their perks.

"I just don't get it," said Jasmyn. "First Kathy and now this."

I stepped closer, looking over Margo's shoulder at a breaking news report. "Someone you know?"

"Not really," said Margo. "Luke Minaker. Kind of a wayward boy; I know the family."

Harold stepped in from the hall. "It's a crying shame."

"It's not the person," said Jasmyn, "it's the way it happened. Kathy drowned without any water anywhere nearby, and now this guy burns to death without anything around him getting so much as a scorch mark. Almost like he burned himself from the inside out."

My jaw dropped, but I think I closed it again before anyone noticed.

Margo glanced at me, then looked back at her computer. "Spontaneous combustion."

"It was murder," said Harold. "Obviously somebody doused him in gas and lit him up. Only way it could happen."

"The police will do an autopsy," I said. The pictures on the website didn't show much, but the general feel was decidedly gruesome.

"I hope they catch the guy that did it and send him straight to hell," said Harold, staring over my shoulder as I stared over Margo's. "He deserves to burn his own self after something like this."

"You don't even know if it was murder," said Jasmyn. "Maybe it was an accident?"

"You ever accidentally burned somebody to death?" asked Harold.

Jasmyn rolled her eyes. "Are you implying that all burn-related deaths are malicious? Come on, Harold, you're killing me. Pun intended."

I let them argue, and sank into my own thoughts. Schrenk's death was suspicious, even before the homeless girl's cryptic warning, but now another death, so similar and yet so mechanically different, in the same town in the same week? They had to be connected. The odds were ridiculous otherwise. Both deaths were unexplained; both deaths were elemental. Could Rain burn people, too? Maybe she didn't just control water, she controlled . . . I don't know, weather? Temperature? But that didn't track with the rest of the Withered I'd met—they weren't X-Men, they were victims of a trade-off: they gave up one thing and lost their humanity, but in its place they gained something else. Lose your body but gain the ability to steal people's bodies. Lose your emotions but gain the ability to feel them in others. What had someone given up, deep in the dawn of history, to gain control over water and fire?

Or . . .

Was it two different Withered?

Rack the Demon King had been raising an army, trying to fight back against our campaign of genocide. Five of them had gathered in Fort Bruce, and the death toll was catastrophic—the news still talked about it, over a year later, though of course they skipped or ignored the supernatural connection. "One of history's most devastating terrorist attacks on American soil." What if Rain was raising her own army? What if Lewisville was hiding a whole host of Withered, ready to pour out vengeance on the frail little humans who had dared to fight back?

"Damn this all to hell," I said.

"Now you're doing it, too," said Jasmyn. "I'm so done with you both."

"What?" I looked up to see Jasmyn fuming and Harold shaking his head. "What did I do?"

"You agreed with me," said Harold. "Jazz hates it when I'm right."

"I hate it when you think you're right," said Jasmyn. "Which is a statistically unlikely amount of the time. You don't know who did this, or if anyone did it at all. You can't pass judgment before you know the facts."

"I think we know enough," I said. "If this was deliberate"—and I knew that it must have been—"then whoever did it is evil. They need to be stopped."

"Men," said Jasmyn. "Stop thinking with your concealed carry permits. Not everyone is evil."

"That doesn't mean everyone's good," I said.

"Obviously not," she said. "But it does mean that everyone's worth saving."

"That I'll agree with," I said, and looked back at the news article. Saving people was the whole reason I was here.

But it looked like I had to save them from a far bigger problem than I'd realized.

CHAPTER 3

Margo and Harold got me situated in the side room, which turned out to be a tiny little ten-by-ten closet off the side of the parking lot. It had a bed on one wall and a dresser on the other, and barely room to turn around in other than that. But it was clean, and it had a roof and two doors that locked, and it was mine. I hadn't had my own place to sleep since Fort Bruce, now more than a year ago.

I locked the doors, sat on the bed, closed my eyes, and listened to the silence.

It was getting dark, but I needed my things so I went back out and sat by the bus stop, reading the little sign and hoping they had nighttime service. It looked like they did. After about ten minutes the bus picked me up. I fed my dollar into the machine and sat by the window, watching as the sun sank over the low hills outside of town, turning the sky pink and yellow and orange and red. It looked like a painting, and then it was gone. The sun disappeared, and the reds turned blue, and I got off at the bus station and pulled my backpack out of my locker. It was dusty from so many rides in the back of so many trucks, and I wondered how long it would be before I ended up in another one, leaving Lewisville behind like I left everything.

Maybe this would be the last one. Maybe Rain and her army were the last Withered left, and I could kill them all and then . . . what? Where would I go next? Not back to Clayton, despite what my sister wanted. That would just mean going back to the FBI, and they'd already tried to arrest me once. I needed to start a new life somewhere.

All I did was start new lives. Over and over.

I found a bus schedule and looked for the seven line back to Ottessen Brothers, but on my way to the bench to wait I saw an electric board that listed seven service as discontinued for the night. Something about a delay or a mechanical failure. I took a breath and rubbed my eyes. The mortuary was five miles away.

Oh well. I'd walked farther than that before and probably would again.

Lewisville felt big to me, though I knew that it wasn't.

It wasn't even as big as Fort Bruce. But I'd grown up in Clayton, which was so small we only had one elementary school—plenty of places only have one high school, but when you only have one elementary, you're tiny. Lewisville had about twenty-nine thousand people, according to the population sign I'd seen when I rode into town, which wasn't enough to put it on anyone's radar, but was big enough. They had a regional airport and a junior college, and they were near enough to some desert canyons to make it at least semipopular as a destination for hikers and mountain bikers. Even with the sun down, the roads were still busy—cars and vans and every kind of pickup truck all gliding through the neon reflections of storefronts and restaurants and old motels. I retraced my steps along the route the bus had taken, which probably wasn't the most direct route back to the mortuary, but at least I knew it well enough to not get lost.

It was only after the first mile or so that I started to wonder if I was being followed.

The biggest city I'd ever been in was Dallas, and in a crowd like that it was impossible to tell if that guy a few blocks behind you was the same guy who'd been there a few minutes ago. Here it was more obvious: other people came and went in brief spurts, crossing the street or walking to or from their cars, but the guy behind me was a constant for most of a mile. I stopped at a streetlight and looked behind me, trying to get a good look as he moved through pools of light: tall, middle-aged, and balding, with a light brown coat that looked like a prop from a truck commercial. Who wore a coat in Arizona in the summer? My light turned green, and I crossed the street quickly. Was I just being paranoid? No one even knew I was in town, or who I was, or why I mattered. He hadn't been at the viewing. But that homeless woman had, and she'd known me, or at least she'd known about me. Somebody, somehow, was aware of my mission. Which meant this guy, if he wasn't just some random guy, was a Withered.

Would a fire-based Withered need a coat in the summer? Did that make any sense at all?

I stopped for another light and looked back again. He was still there, and closer.

And talking to someone I couldn't see. I couldn't hear him, but his mouth was moving almost constantly.

I had to consider the possibility that he was a completely different Withered I didn't know about yet. If Rain was gathering an army, who knew how many there were in town?

I reached another corner and on a whim, turned left, away from the main drag. If he still followed me here then it wasn't a coincidence; he was definitely following me. I realized I was holding my breath and forced myself to breathe normally. I walked past a car dealership bathed in light, and then beyond it to a row of brick apartments and repair shops that were smothered in darkness which was broken only by a handful of scattered street lamps. Two blocks later the road ended at a wide dirt parking lot and the edge of a canal rimmed by a battered chain-link fence. I glanced behind me; the man was still there. Closer than ever.

And I'd brought myself to the middle of nowhere, without any help in sight.

I started running, and the man ran after me. All pretense was gone now. My heavy backpack bounced against my spine, and I tried to figure out where I could go. Would witnesses be enough to deter him, or would I need an actual defense? I was in good shape—I could run—but I wasn't a fighter. That's not how I killed them. I watched them and studied them and found out their weak points, and then used those to make them helpless. I killed with time and secrecy. In a straight-up fight with a grown man, I would inevitably lose.

I risked a look behind me but it was too late—the man was just a few yards back, his footsteps in the gravel melding with mine so I couldn't hear them. He wasn't calling out to me, which meant he wasn't trying to tell me something, but as he drew closer I could hear him still muttering under his breath—short, angry growls between labored gasps for air. I lowered my head and pushed myself harder, trying to reach what looked like a bar or pool hall at the end of the road. But before I could get there, he caught hold of my backpack and yanked it backward; I lost my footing and tumbled to the ground. He jumped on me immediately, kicking me in the side of the head and then dropping to his knees to punch me three times in the stomach. I doubled over in pain, my eyes bursting with light as I reeled from his kick, and I lost track of what was happening. I regained my senses just in time to realize that he had picked me up, and I let out an incoherent cry as he tossed me over the chain link fence. I landed on sharp rocks and thistles and rolled painfully down the hill toward the canal.

"Kill you," the man muttered. "She says I have to kill you."

I groaned in pain, feeling like my arm had broken in the tumble. I heard the fence clank as he jumped over it, and felt a cascade of gravel against my face and arms as he started down the hill toward me. I braced my arms underneath me and pushed myself up; I guess it wasn't broken, then, but it hurt like hell.

"She says I have to kill you," the man repeated.

"Who says?"

He kicked at me again, but the ground was unstable and a rugged bush disrupted his footing, giving me just enough time to throw myself out of the way. I tumbled a few more feet closer to the water, as black as ink in the darkness.

"Who says you have to kill me?" I gasped.

"The Dark Lady," he said. His voice was ragged, like he'd been screaming. He picked his way closer, through the rocks and thorns. "She said I have to do it. She said I have to drown you." He lunged for me, and I tried to move again, but the ground gave way under my feet; I collapsed to the rocks and he clamped his hands down, one on my arm and one on my neck. "I don't want to do it, but she says I have to."

I swung my free hand up to beat at his face, but he ignored it and dragged me down to the edge of the water; I could hear it burbling, an innocent sound made horribly ominous by its inescapable proximity.

"You don't have to kill me." Was the Dark Lady Rain? Did it even matter right now? My face was pressed hard against the rocks, so close to the water I could feel the moisture through the stones.

"She told me I have to."

"Ignore her."

"I can't!" he screamed. He forced me closer to the edge of the canal, millimeter by millimeter. "She's everything!"

I pressed my free arm into the water, bracing myself so he couldn't push me further. "I can help you," I said. "I know what the Dark Lady is—take me to her and I can help you get rid of her."

"I can't stop myself!"

"Hey!" a new voice shouted down from the road above us. And another followed: "What's going on down there?"

"Somebody help me!" The plea came not from my throat, but from my attacker's. "She wants me to kill him!" He shoved me closer to the water, the sharp rocks scraping across my face. I forgot all hope of talking and simply fought back with all my strength, kicking and wriggling and doing everything I could to escape. He slammed my head into the gravel, and then shoved me in the water. Sight and sound seemed to disappear, and I choked on the water that flooded my mouth midscream. I flailed helplessly, my head trapped in an iron grip below the water—and then suddenly the hands that held me disappeared. I exploded out of the water in a desperate lunge, spitting out filth and gasping for air. A cluster of figures stood around me, and I struck at them blindly, but one of them caught my arms.

"Easy, pal, easy. We're here to help you."

"What?"

Another man grabbed my backpack and hauled me up onto dry land. I smelled smoke. Something was beating at the water, splashing wildly in the middle of the canal.

"He ran away when we got down here," said the man beside me. "Dove right in the water before we could grab him." Strong hands slapped me on the back, and I coughed up more water. "You okay?"

I coughed again. "I think so." My attacker reached the other side of the canal and climbed up on the opposite bank.

"Bastard got away," said another man. "What was he doing, trying to kill you?"

"I don't know," I said. Could I tell them the truth? "Just mug me, I think."

"You gotta watch out in this neighborhood," said a man.

"You get a good look at him?" said another. "I'm calling the cops, you can give 'em a statement."

"No," I said quickly, easing myself to my feet. "No cops." If this was a Withered, I'd rather investigate it myself—not to mention that I didn't have any ID. "It was nothing, we don't need to report this, I'm fine."

"You nuts?"

"I'm fine," I said again. I tried to see my rescuers in the moonlight, but it was too dark to make out anything more than a few pale silhouettes. At least one of them was dressed like a biker, and I guessed that they'd come from the bar I hadn't quite reached in my sprint to escape. "I'd rather not, um, get the law involved in this."

The man beside me grew suddenly wary. "You mixed up in drugs or something?"

"It's not that," I said, "I just don't have any ID, you know?" Maybe they'd understand drifting, if nothing else. "Just staying off the grid."

"I hear that," said another man. "Come on, let's get you back up to the road."

They helped me up the hill, and the climb convinced me that I hadn't broken anything. I was soaked, though, and probably scraped all to pieces. They walked me to the bar, and I got a better look at them—all adult men, all from various walks of blue-collar life. They tried to buy me some food to warm me up, but all the bar had was hot wings, so I ate the carrot sticks and assured them that I was fine. I could walk, and I had a place to stay. They gradually accepted my thanks, and when they finally wandered back to their own disparate business I left the bar and walked the rest of the way back to the mortuary. No one followed me.

It wasn't until I reached my room and stripped off my wet clothes that I saw the back of my backpack:

Two handprints, right where one of the men had grabbed it to pull me from the canal, burned into the nylon fabric, as clear as day.

CHAPTER 4

There is a subset of serial killers called the "visionary killers": men and women who kill not out of greed or hunger or vengeance or lust or anything else that drives us, but because they believe that a higher power told them to. David Berkowitz, better known as the Son of Sam, was one of these. He killed eight women in New York City in the summer of 1976. He believed that his neighbor Sam was a demon, sending messages through a dog, forcing Berkowitz to kill. He didn't want to—he sent letters to the police begging them to stop him—but what else was he going to do? The dog told him to kill, so he killed. There was nothing he could do about it.

Another visionary killer was a man named Herbert Mullin, who heard voices telling him that the Earth needed blood sacrifice to prevent a devastating earthquake. He called this "singing the die song," and believed that some of the voices came from his father, some from heaven, and some from the victims themselves. He didn't want to kill, but if he didn't then the whole continent would fall into the ocean and millions more would die instead. When the voices told him to kill, he killed. And there was nothing he could do about it.

And now a man had tried to kill me.

What if the Dark Lady my attacker had talked about was Rain? What if she was a Withered with some kind of mind control, who drowned people not through some crazy, impossible, supernatural method, but simply by telling this man to drown people in the canal, and then return them to their homes? Why? Who knows? Obviously they gained something valuable by doing so. The problem that made Withered so hard to hunt was that the things they gained were so different, and through such different means, than a regular human. The first one I'd met, my neighbor Mr. Crowley, had been replacing his failing body parts by stealing them from other people. How was a police officer with no knowledge of the supernatural supposed to figure that out?

And how did the fire fit into it? My backpack had two perfect handprints burned into it, a right and a left, but the man who attacked me had never grabbed my backpack with both hands—his left hand had always been solidly on my neck. The man who'd used two hands had been one of my rescuers. Had I been saved from one Withered by another one? Had he known what he was doing? Had either of them known who I was? Then why hadn't he identified himself? Or was it all some implausible coincidence?

I needed to find them. I'd gotten a brief look at my attacker, at least from a distance, and I'd seen all four of my rescuers up close. Was only one of them a Withered, or were they all working together? What in the bloody hell was going on in Lewisville?

I couldn't just run off and spend the day looking. I had a job now, and I needed to keep it if I wanted to maintain my access to the dead bodies that were sure to start appearing all over the city. I had to keep Margo happy, and that meant I had to be a model employee.

One of the two doors in my side room led outside, and the other led into the mortuary. I let myself in early the next morning and showered in the back room before getting dressed and showing myself around. It was hard to move after the last night's beating, but my bruises were all covered by clothes or my longish hair, so at least I wouldn't have to answer any hard questions. The mortuary had a different layout than the one I'd grown up in, but even so, it was achingly familiar. The chapel, the embalming room, even the supply closet was a tangible, almost delectable reminder of my life growing up, and the times

I'd spent in silence and solitude, carefully grooming the dead on their way to whatever awaited them beyond the grave. I hoped it was nothing, because that was exactly what I longed for: silence, blackness, and peace. An end to all trouble.

I pulled Kathy Schrenk's body out of the refrigerator and examined it, looking for any evidence I could find of how she had died, or that suggested a Withered might have done it, but I didn't see anything. I double-checked everything, just to be sure, even going so far as to cut a few slits on the body's back to take a look at the pooled, dead blood, but there was nothing out of the ordinary. I shook my head and put her back in the fridge. It was almost time for the workday to start, and there was no sense being caught messing with corpses on my very first day on the job. I found the custodial closet, neatly arranged, and got to work in the embalming room, wiping down all the counters and scrubbing all the tools until they shined. I washed the tables, the walls, and the handles on the doors, and was halfway through a meticulous mopping of the floor when Margo arrived.

"Morning, Robert."

"Morning," I said.

She surveyed the spotless room and nodded, obviously satisfied but seeing no apparent need to state it out loud. "When you're done in here, help me out in the chapel. Kathy's funeral's at noon."

We vacuumed the chapel and dusted the pews and

curtains, and when Jasmyn arrived she and I washed the windows while Margo finalized and printed a stack of paper programs, folding them in half with a ruler for a crisp, perfect edge. Harold arrived at 10:30 with flowers, and Kathy's family a few minutes later—no husband or children, as she'd had none, only the one sister, just as single as Kathy had been. Carol Schrenk. They'd been twins, like my mom and my aunt, and I helped as she and Margo gave the final, reverent touches to Kathy's hair and makeup and clothing. At eleven I went back to my room to change into my suit, only to realize that I'd still been wearing it when the Dark Lady's acolyte had thrown me into the canal, and it was still torn and muddy. I found my best jeans and my only other collared shirt and hoped that Lewisville was enough of a redneck town for that to count as fancy clothes. Margo frowned when she saw me, but nearly half of the men who arrived for the funeral were wearing the same, so I fit in well enough.

"I don't want you to fit in," said Margo, taking me aside. "You're an employee of my mortuary, and I want you to stand out as a formal and respectful representative of that business."

"My suit got a little messed up," I said. "First paycheck I get, I'll buy a new one."

"I can find you a new one," she grumbled. "Just next time give me some warning."

Jasmyn and I stood in the back while Carol gave a tepid eulogy, and then an ancient friend of Kathy's stood up

to give a warbling rendition of "You'll Never Walk Alone."
At the end, Margo stood up to give some closing remarks,
which apparently she never does. Jasmyn's jaw practically
dropped to the floor.

"I suppose you could say that most of these funerals are
for friends of mine," said Margo. "I probably shouldn't get
up and talk at any of them, but Kathy was an employee,
and a good one, and I respect that." She held the sides of
the lectern—not tightly, like she needed it for support, but
firmly, almost as if the lectern needed her. "Kathy never
missed a day of work when it counted. She had a way of
knowing, like some kind of sixth sense, exactly when we'd
be busy and when we wouldn't, and somehow she managed to be healthy on all the right days. Kept your friends
and neighbors looking pretty for their funerals. She was
here when you needed her." Margo looked out over the
audience, and I thought she might be searching for somebody specific. She didn't find the person, and sighed. "But
all things have to end eventually, I guess. We just do the
best we can until it happens." She paused again. "Thanks
for coming. We'll see you at the cemetery."

In the movies it's always raining at the cemetery, and
everyone's dressed in black with big black umbrellas. We
drove there in the scorching Arizona sun and stood by the
grave while the wind whipped curled flurries of dust
around our feet. The open grave was surrounded by green
carpets of fake grass and topped with a lowering device:
an open metal frame with a pair of straps across the middle

to support the casket. My mom always used to make fun of the name—couldn't they come up with something better than "lowering device"—but it never bothered me. What else were they going to call it? It was a device that lowered caskets. A few feet away, the cemetery had set out twenty or thirty folding chairs, and the small crowd of mourners sat in the sun and the wind while a local pastor said some basic stuff about life and death, and then ended with a prayer.

Why do we do graveside services? We just got out of the funeral literally fifteen minutes ago; we've said all the same things, spouted all the same trite homilies, invoked all the same blessings of all the same deities. It's unnecessary, but I suppose that's not the same thing as being pointless. We're human beings—we need ceremony. We need to commemorate things. Just as I liked to brush a dead body's hair, trim its nails, and prepare it for the end, other people liked to stand by the grave and bid the body farewell.

The pastor prayed, and the sister cried, and Jasmyn put her hair into a bun with a pen from her back pocket, and the groundskeeper waited about forty yards away, leaning on the side of a faded yellow backhoe and sipping a soda from a fat white cup from a gas station. The wind blew, and the clouds moved, and somewhere in the distance trucks hurried down a highway. The graveside service ended, the mourners trickled away, and I cranked the lever on the lowering device so the bars in the frame turned, and the straps unspooled, and the casket lowered into the cement box waiting at the bottom of the hole. When it reached the bottom we disconnected the straps from one side of the frame and pulled them out the other side; the casket sat on raised bumps in the box, so the straps could slide out easily from underneath it. We stowed the lowering device and the folding chairs in a flatbed truck, and pulled away the green carpets to expose the bare dirt around the top of the grave. I rolled them carefully, keeping the dull red dirt from smearing the clean top surface. The groundskeeper brought the backhoe, lowered the lid of the cement box down into the grave, then threw his empty soda cup in after it and started filling the hole with dirt. Harold and Margo rode home in the hearse while Jasmyn drove me in her car. We never said a word.

At the mortuary Harold handed me a black suit, used, but clean and my size. "Margo said you needed this."

"Thanks. That was fast."

"I live to serve." He tipped an imaginary hat, and we cleaned up the chapel again.

I went back to the bar where my rescuers had taken me the night before, but without their company or any ID, the bartender wouldn't let me in. I told him I wanted to reward the men for saving my life, which he thought was a nice gesture. Since it was still too early for any real crowd, he stood in the doorway and answered my questions. He could remember most of the men, as they were regulars, but one in particular was new. I focused on that one.

"Do you know the man's name?"

The bartender shook his head. "Nope."

"What do you call him, then?"

He tucked his shaggy hair behind his ears. "I just call everyone 'boss,' then I don't have to know their names."

"Okay. Do you know how long he's been in town?"

"Three, four days at the most. He's probably coming back tonight if you want to leave him a message."

"Do you mind if I just hang out here in front and wait for him? For all of them?"

The bartender shrugged. "Long as you don't do drugs or anything that'll get me in trouble."

"Scout's honor."

"Thank you, boss. Good luck."

He shook my hand and went back inside. I sat on the bench by the front door for a few minutes, waiting, then decided to walk back down the road a bit to the place where the visionary killer had tried to drown me. I couldn't find it. I'd thought maybe I might be able to identify the spot by some damage to the fence, or to the weeds on the slope, but it all looked the same in the light. I walked back to the bar and waited, and as each man came to the door I thanked him and shook his hand, and asked if he could remember anything about the man who'd attacked me. None of them could recall his face, though they all

remembered the coat pretty clearly. One of them identified it by make and style—it was a popular choice among
local ranchers, apparently—but that was the best they
could do.

Around eight o'clock, as the sky was just darkening
to twilight, the last man arrived at the bar. The out-of-
towner. He was about as tall as I was, but stocky and
hairy, with a long black beard and a head of long hair
pulled back in a ponytail. He wore a black T-shirt with
what I assume was a band logo, but I didn't recognize it. I
stood up and shook his hand, introducing myself as the
kid from last night.

"Oh, hey," he said, and shook my hand vigorously.
His hand was warm, and I felt a sense of sudden terror
that I would burst into flames at his touch. "How you
doin'?"

"I'm fine," I said, "thank you. I wanted to say thank you
again for helping me out."

"It's no problem," he said, and gestured toward the
door. "You want a drink?"

"No thank you," I said. "Do you mind if I ask you some
questions?"

He looked longingly at the door, but shrugged. "I guess
not. What can I do for you?"

I had a handful of methods I could try, hoping to get
information from him, but I decided to start with the
simple one first: "Did you see the guy who attacked me?
His face, I mean?"

The man leaned against the wall and puffed out his cheeks as he talked. "Not really. Balding, but not all the way—he had some hair back there. Blond, mostly, but darkish blond. Not Swedish blond or anything, you know? Kind of stubbly beard, too, but I think that might have been coming in red, like they do sometimes—one color up top, different color on the face."

That was more detail than anyone else had given me. "What about his coat?"

"Yeah, I think he had a coat on."

I nodded, wondering what his vastly different recollections of the event might mean. If anything. "What else can you remember?"

"Why do you ask? You're not going to go looking for him, are you?"

That was also strange—the other men had assumed I had come to my senses and was getting ready to approach the police, and so I was trying to put together a mental image to give a good description. This guy thought I was taking matters into my own hands. Did that mean anything? Did any of it?

I tried a new tactic. "I, um, want to give you guys a reward. Not something fancy, because I can't afford much, but still a little something, just like a . . . thing. Is it way creepy of me to ask for your address, so I have somewhere to take it once I get it?"

"Probably," he said, laughing. "But I don't have an address. I don't live here, I'm really just passing through."

"Me too," I said. "Hitchhiking?"

"No," he said, "I've got a car; I just don't really have much of anything else."

Now we were getting somewhere. "What brings you through Lewisville, then? I'm only here because I couldn't get a ride anywhere else."

"Got a friend in town."

That had to be Rain. "What's that address?" I asked. "I could bring the thing there."

"You can just bring it here," he said. "That's fine." He straightened up from his slump against the wall. "I'm glad I could help you, man, but I'm gonna head inside."

Crap. I had to pull out the big guns. "What's your name?"

He opened the door. "Saul."

"I mean your real name," I said, and then I threw all caution to the wind. "The one Rain used when she called you."

He stopped, turned, and looked at me.

I looked back, trying to be brave. Nothing I'd ever seen suggested that the Withered could sense each other's presence.

"Rain?" he asked.

"That's the only name I know her by," I said. "I assume she used to have a different one, because we all did, but . . . I honestly can't even remember mine."

He studied me for a moment and then spoke softly. "Meshara?"

That was Elijah's name—a Withered with no memory. I shook my head. "No, he died in Fort Bruce."

"That's what I figured," the man murmured.

There was only one Withered I could reasonably fake. "I'm Nobody," I said. I'd hunted her for weeks and lived with her, through Brooke, for over a year. I swallowed and watched the man's reaction, hoping he'd believe me.

"Been a while since you took a boy," he said at last.

I nodded, trying not to show my relief that he believed me. "I know." I hadn't actually known that Nobody had ever taken a male body, but it was a safe guess. Ten thousand years is a very long time.

He looked at me a while, then nodded, as if satisfying some mental checklist that I was indeed an ageless, bodiless monster. "I'm Assu. The God of the Sun. Let's go inside and get a beer."

CHAPTER 5

"I've mostly been bumming around," said Assu. He sipped beer from his brown-glass bottle, and when he set it back down on the coaster he carefully positioned it precisely on top of the moisture ring where it had sat before. "Shoveling coal," he said, "back when that was a thing. Smelting ore, off and on, but I never liked doing that much. Just because you can do something doesn't mean you enjoy it, right?"

"You know me," I said, trying to say what Nobody would say. "I never enjoy anything."

"Not for long, anyway." He took another sip. "Sure you don't want one?"

"This body doesn't drink."

Assu raised an eyebrow. "And you care what your body does and doesn't do? How long are you even going to keep this one?"

Nobody had committed suicide so many times she'd lost track. Thousands and thousands. I wondered, then, if Brooke had been Nobody longer than anybody else had ever been. Unless that homeless girl from the viewing had been Nobody? I still didn't know, and I didn't even know how to find her. Assu was the only lead I had, so I had to keep him talking. "I guess I'll keep this one as long as I can."

"Well, good luck to you," he said. "How about a burger?"

"Vegetarian."

Assu laughed. "What is this, method acting?"

I was acting too much like myself, and he was getting suspicious. I thought of a defense that could maybe explain it. "Do you switch bodies?" I asked.

"Nope," he said. "This is the only one I've got."

"Then you wouldn't understand," I said, as if that explained the issue. More important, though, was his admission: if Assu didn't body-swap, then I could kill this one and he'd die forever . . . once I'd figured out how, of course. And once I'd gotten what I needed from him. I turned the conversation back to the information I was trying to learn. "Have you been to see Rain yet?"

"Not yet," he said. "I figure she knows I'm here, after

that body I left her a few days ago. Luke Minaker." He took another sip. "Let her stew for a while; I don't need her drama."

"It's the end of the world," I said. "Or our world, at least. Some drama seems justified."

"I guess it is," he said. "Probably time, though, don't you think?"

"For drama?" This was more introspective than most of the Withered I'd met had ever gotten.

He shook his head. "For endings."

I thought about this for a moment, trying to think of a response. Once again, I had to think like Nobody to come up with a good one. "Endings aren't as great as you think they are," I said. "I've done it plenty of times."

"That's the problem, though, isn't it? Your endings don't count because your endings never stick. You keep ending *them*, and never yourself. To hear Rain tell it now, the whole human race is all coming out of the woodwork trying to end us. Which is the exact opposite of your regular situation, so you don't have much of a leg to stand on." He took another pull on his beer and flagged down the waitress to order a ham sandwich with onion rings. "So you can have some veggies," he told me, watching the girl's butt as she walked away. "You ever . . . You ever been a waitress?"

"Yeah."

"You ever hear any pickup lines that totally worked on you?"

I raised my eyebrow. "Ten thousand years old and you need help picking up a small-town waitress?"

"Bah," he said, and drained his beer. He clunked it down solidly on the tabletop. "I know being hypercritical is your whole thing, but can you keep it to yourself? I don't need it right now."

"Fine," I said, and looked around the bar. "You think they have a jukebox here?"

"Every crappy bar has a jukebox," he said. "And they all have crappy songs."

"Probably," I said. "I didn't want to listen to one anyway. Just making small talk."

"You suck at it."

"So I've been told."

Assu leaned back in his chair, resting his arm on the back of the chair next to him. "What were you the god of? Goddess, whatever."

"I've been both," I said. "I assume."

"You don't remember?"

"You've lived ten thousand years," I said. All the Withered had. "I've lived ten thousand lives, at least. Maybe a hundred thousand. And every one of them comes with its own memories. There's so much backstory bouncing around in this head it's a wonder I can even tie my own shoes in the morning."

"Makes sense," he said, and then chuckled. "You remember that? When they invented shoes?"

"Shoes are one of the oldest inventions of human civilization," I said.

"I know, I know" he said. "But I'm talking about modern shoes—like, when they started making them comfortable, instead of just leather sandals and junk like that. The first time you ever put on sneakers and felt that cushy sole, tied those nylon laces, and it all just fits perfectly, for the first time in your whole long life."

What a weird thing to remember. I shook my head. "Everybody I've taken either never had good shoes or always had them. I guess I missed that particular experience."

"It's never really been your feet anyway," he said. "Has it?"

"Not really."

"Does that bother you?"

I saw him looking at me, just out of the corner of his eye, trying to look like he wasn't paying attention but still somehow concerned about the answer. I took the cue and considered my answer carefully.

What would Nobody have said? Did it bother her not to have her own body? Probably; sooner or later everything bothered Nobody, which is why she'd kept killing herself and moving on. But the bodies she'd killed, like he said, had never really been hers. They'd been clothing that she picked up and discarded, without ever really thinking about the realities of their lives.

But no, that wasn't true. Nobody, like Elijah, was filled with human memory; she'd seen us differently than the other Withered because she'd lived *as* us instead of simply among us. She knew our dreams because they'd been hers, and she knew our realities because she'd never been able to face them. A girl always looked beautiful from a distance, like a doll or a marble statue: a thing we admire without ever getting to know. Until you get to know her. Get up close and she's as real as anyone else. Girls have flaws and hang-ups and odors and every other problem that everyone has ever had. That was what had bothered Nobody, I think: truth. The world's stubborn refusal to be a fairy tale, or a girl to be a fairy princess.

"I had feet once," I said.

"You sound like a backwards Little Mermaid," said Assu.

A fairy tale. Because of course.

"Maybe I was," I said. Nobody had only ever wanted the things she couldn't have, and she'd made a devil's bargain to get them. "I had feet, and a body, and everything." I pointed at the other patrons in the bar. "Anything any of them ever had. But then we gave it all up and I lost them, and I think . . ." I paused. What would Nobody say? What did she think about the body she'd given up? "I think the body I had was the only one I could have ever been happy in."

"But you hated it."

"I did," I said. "And now here I am."

Assu looked around the bar, his eyes solemn. "Not exactly the life we'd imagined, is it?"

"No, it's not," I said, and it was as true for me as for Nobody.

The waitress came back, setting down the sandwich and rings and a fresh beer. The cap sat on the top, half on and bent in the middle; the mouth of the bottle smoked gently as the cold moisture condensed in the hot belly of the bar.

"Here you go, boys," she said, and Assu smiled.

"Thank you," he said. "Hey, um, what was your name?"

"Lara, honey. You need something?"

"Lara," said Assu, "do you have a . . . ? I mean, what time do you get off work?"

"I'm sorry, hon," she said. "We're not allowed to date the customers. Can I get you anything else?"

Assu looked defeated, and his voice was hollow. "Just some ice."

"Sure thing." She walked away, and he stared at his sandwich.

I didn't know what to say, so I simply sat and watched him.

"Do you remember wonder?" he asked.

"Wonder?"

"Awe," he said. "Joy. Surprise." He poked at his sandwich but didn't pick it up. "Do you remember the last time you saw something for the first time? The first time you saw the ocean, or ate a spicy pepper, or kissed someone? The first time you heard a wolf pack howling in the dark, the whole group of them just howling and howling, calling and answering, and the sound going up and out and disappearing? Maybe an echo, maybe not. Ten thousand years—and maybe two, three hundred years of it had wonder, and then eventually you'd seen it all, or felt it all, or done it all. And then you had fun for a few thousand more just doing it all again—finding that one delicious food that you couldn't get enough of, and eating it and eating it in all its different forms. And then, eventually, you've done everything. And you've done it a thousand times. And what's the point of doing it again? I know what this ham sandwich is going to taste like because I've eaten more ham sandwiches than one man can ever possibly appreciate. It's just fuel, now, stoking the fire and keeping me alive. And why?"

I watched him as he stared into the past; watched the beer bottle as the smoky condensation rose up from the crooked cap. "You've had ham," I said, "but you've never had this ham."

"What's the difference?" he asked. "This ham, this bar, this waitress. Are they really going to be new in any meaningful way?"

"Not the ham," I admitted. "The people, though. I mean, that's what they say, right? That we're all little snowflakes, perfectly individual and unique."

"And yet every snowstorm looks the same," he said. "Every single time."

The waitress came back with a glass full of ice, set it on

the table with a wink, and walked away. Assu picked up the glass, and the ice cubes started melting at his touch, slowly trickling down into the bottom of the glass. He dumped them into his other hand, and they disappeared in midair, dissolving into liquid and mist bare millimeters before touching his skin. Water ran on the floor, and steam rose up from his hand, and he stared at it with ancient eyes.

There was only one thing to say. "You gave up cold."

His voice was a whisper: "It's the only thing in the world I can't feel."

He watched the steam rise from his hand, until it was completely dry. Then he spoke again in a voice so soft I had to lean in close to hear him. "When I was a boy," he said, "out on the foothills out where we lived, by the old village—do you remember it?"

"I don't."

"It was beautiful," he said. "But it was harsh. I think that's why we did so well, or why our parents did so well. And their parents and their parents and all the way back: they couldn't just coast, in a place like that, so they built and they created and they *did*. They herded sheep—for all I know they *invented* herding sheep—and one day, when I was a boy, the winter came early, and I was caught in a storm on the slopes of the mountain in the high grazing ranges. I was dressed for the cold—it wasn't *that* sudden—but not for a storm like that, and I tried to bring the sheep home, but the snow blocked the passes and hid the trails, and I was trapped. I built a hut, and I built a fire, but it just kept snowing and snowing and snowing, and the food ran out and the water froze solid, and my blankets froze with it, and I huddled in the middle of the sheep for warmth. I guess it was enough because I didn't die, but only barely. And I swore that I would never be cold again, and I lived in the desert, and I cursed the night sky and the winds that came down off the mountain. And then when Rain came to us, and Rack told us of his plan, I gave up all cold, and all cold feelings. In return I gained more heat and flame than any other body could hold: the power to scorch the sands and wither the plants and to shine like the sun itself." He put his hand on the empty glass, which began to glow yellow in his grip. "I lived as a god—of the sun and the forge, and of bronze, and iron, and steel." The yellow glow turned red, and the glass began to droop, and he squeezed it in his hand like a film of shining clay, squeezing it into a tight, dense rope the width of his fist, and it grew hotter and brighter until it poured down across his hand, and dripped on the table, singeing the wood. It all ran down, and the table smoked and burned, and he opened his hand for the last few drops to fall away. The pool of glass glowed red, cooling slowly. A couple of the other bar patrons were staring at us, wondering where that bitter scent of scorched wood had come from.

I had no words. Assu pulled a money clip from his back pocket, peeled off a couple of bills, and dropped them on the table.

"Let's go," he said, and stood up.

I stood with him, trying to force myself to speak. What had just happened? I knew the what—but *why* had it just happened? What had Assu felt, or decided, that had put him into this dark mood? "Where are we going?" I asked.

"Somewhere cold," he said, and turned to go. "A restaurant, maybe, or a butcher. Somewhere with one of those big, walk-in freezers."

I hurried after him. "But you can't feel it."

"That doesn't mean I have to stop trying." He walked outside, into the hot night air and spat angrily on the ground. "Damn woman. Brought me here to this hell. She can fight her own damn war."

"So let's go tell her," I said. I needed him to focus—to tell me where Rain was so I could find this Withered army and stop them once and for all. "Let's go find her right now, and tell her off, and see what she's planning. Then you can go straight back to Alaska or Siberia or wherever you were before, and be done with her forever. But let's at least find her."

"No."

"Come on," I said.

"Do you work for her?" He spun on me suddenly, pressing me against the wall of the bar with his hands. I could feel the heat from his palms and his fingers. I shook my head.

"No."

"Then help me," he said. "Cold first, and then Rain."

"Okay," I said. "Cold first." I hesitated. "I think I know the perfect place."

The mortuary was empty at night; Harold had an apartment next door, but my little room was the only one that accessed the building directly. Assu parked his car, and I used my key to let him in—through my room and into the heart of the building. I kept the lights off, guiding him by feel and memory into the embalming room at the back. This room had no external windows, so I closed the door, and clicked on the light, and gestured to the giant metal fridge against the wall.

"A freezer?" he asked.

"Sometimes," I said. "We can set the controls. There's nobody in there right now—the burn victim hasn't come in yet, so we don't have any bodies. We can set the temperature as low as you want."

"As low as it'll go," he said.

A mortuary fridge has multiple little doors, each with a metal plate that rolls out like a bed, like you see in the morgues on TV. This fridge had six. Assu opened the top door and we pulled out the plate, and he laid himself down on it, headfirst. "As cold as it will go," he said, and I slid him in until all I could see were the soles of his shoes.

The fridge in my parents' mortuary had had a little dial,

but this one had a keypad. It only went down to one degree Celsius; I hoped that would be enough for him.

"Close the door," he said.

"You'll suffocate."

"That's not how it works," he said. "Close the door."

I closed it and waited. What was he doing? Just lying there? What did he think was going to happen?

"Assu," I shouted. "Can you hear me?"

His voice was faint, but I could make it out: "Yes."

"Is it cold?"

"How the hell would I know?"

I shrugged and leaned against the wall. How long was he going to be in there?

How many times had he tried this exact thing, in a thousand other refrigerators and freezers, only to get frustrated when he couldn't feel cold?

I waited. It wasn't the weirdest thing I'd ever done in a mortuary. As long as he eventually led me to Rain, he could lay in the fridge as long as he wanted.

Five minutes later, the rubber insulation around the door started melting.

I saw it first as a sag—the rubber seal was drooping down from the bottom of the fridge door, though it hadn't yet separated from the metal. A moment later it sagged enough that the seal broke, and smoke from inside poured out in massive billows. I barely had time to think and reacted on pure instinct: there was a fire inside, and it had just gotten a burst of new oxygen, and it was about to explode. I threw myself to the side, racing out of the way, and in that moment the door of the refrigeration chamber blew off and a giant gout of flame roared out. The bulletin board against the far wall charred almost instantly, the papers curling into black coal tendrils. The wall scorched, the paint bubbling and peeling away. I felt a moment of perfect joy—a fire was free!—and then the sprinklers in the ceiling burst into life, and the room was soaked, and reality came crashing back down again. The flames on the wall traveled upward, and the heat in the room was still shockingly fierce, but the flames in the fridge disappeared. I crept back around to the front of the refrigeration unit, wondering what I would see, but I already knew. I peered inside, and there it was: a puddle of thick, greasy ash, black and flaky, and bubbling and hissing. Soulstuff.

Assu was dead, and the mortuary was burning.

CHAPTER 6

Fire licked at the walls and the ceiling, defying the sprinklers and spreading hungrily through the mortuary, inches from my back and eventually, inevitably, blocking all the exits, trapping me inside. In hindsight, I should have been afraid for my life, or exulting in the flames, or maybe even both, but instead my thoughts were laser-focused on one simple, horrible fact:

The firefighters would come, and the police, and they'd report on the blaze, and that report would include the soulstuff. "Unidentifiable black sludge." Intelligence analysts for the FBI would see it, and they'd recognize it for what it was, and they'd come. And they'd find me.

And everything I had would be taken away.

I looked at the sludge in the fridge unit, still smoldering on the metal slab. It would be way too hot to touch. I looked around for something to absorb the heat, like a blanket or a sheet—embalming rooms usually had plenty of those—but nothing in this room would help because all of it was wet, and heat moved too freely through wet fabric. I looked around for something else I could use, but most things in a mortuary are designed to protect from chemicals and cold, not heat.

Except one thing. I ran to the door and threw it open, flipping on all the lights as I passed them—the fire alarm had already gone off, and the firefighters would be here soon, so there was no point in hiding my presence anymore. I raced to the cremation room, grabbed the thermal apron and hand mitts, and ran back. How much time did I have? I pulled on the clothes as I ran, and gritted my teeth as I ran past a spot in the hall where the flames were licking through the wall, and suddenly all the sprinklers in the hall came on and I was caught in another downpour. I plunged back into the embalming room, grabbed a mop bucket, and ran to the open fridge. I pulled out the metal slab carefully, trying not to spill the sludge; it was thick, and didn't run much, so I pulled out about a foot of it and scraped the gunk off the slab and into the bucket, where it hissed and popped like frying oil. I could feel the heat of it even through the cremation mitts. I cleared the first bit of sludge and pulled out the slab another foot. Some of it fell on the floor, narrowly missing my foot, and I told myself to come back for it later, concentrating everything I could on the sludge on the table. I pulled the slab out farther and farther, sweeping the sludge into the bucket; I could feel the bucket heating up and wondered how long I had before the soulstuff melted a hole in it.

I could hear the sirens in the distance and raced to finish. I scraped all the last bits of gunk into the bucket, rubbing at the metal frantically with the mitts, trying to get every last drop. It was obvious the fire had started in the fridge, so maybe if there were only a few bits left they'd think it was an accelerant for an arson attack?

Dammit. Who would they blame for arson? Maybe the homeless drifter kid they knew nothing about? I couldn't think about that yet—hide the sludge first, then worry about everything else.

The refrigeration chamber held a handful of metal bits that hadn't burned with Assu's body and clothes, and I tried to grab those as well: some buttons and rivets from his jeans, and a ring with some keys, and a scattering of blackened coins. I dumped them all in the bucket and ran for the door—but stopped, ran back, and scraped wildly at the floor. Could I get it all up in time? I smeared the sticky sludge across the mitts, dropped them in the bucket, and ran again for the door. The sirens were closer, but I couldn't tell how close. I heard the lock on the back door jiggle, probably Harold trying to get in, and sprinted to the front door, kicking my way out and then running around to the parking lot. I needed to get rid of Assu's car, too—if the cops saw it here at the scene of the fire, they'd start asking questions, which would lead to the bar, and the bartender, and me. Always back to me. I used the edge of the cremation apron to fish Assu's car key out of the bucket, and I tried it gingerly with my hand; it was scalding hot, but I had no other choice, so I shoved it into the door to unlock it. The fire truck had already arrived at the front of the building, but no one was back here yet. I opened the car door and threw the bucket into the passenger's seat. The sludge on the key made it stick in the lock, but I managed to wrench it out and climbed into the car, slamming the key into the ignition and turning it wildly. The engine roared to life, and I peeled out of the parking lot without turning on the lights.

I drove in the dark for a few blocks, then turned the lights on and drove farther into town, looking for some place to dump the car and the stuff in it. I passed a grocery store, closed at this hour, pulled into the lot behind it and parked next to their big metal Dumpster. Being careful not to spill any soulstuff on the car or my clothes, I pulled out the bucket and the cremation clothes and placed them carefully in the Dumpster, using some of the garbage to cover it. With the sludge hidden, I got back in the car and drove away again, looking for somewhere to stash the vehicle itself. I settled on a motel parking lot, hoping that it might be able to sit there for a few days without drawing any special attention. I used my shirt to wipe down everything I'd touched: the steering wheel, the shifter, the door handles. I got out, closed the door, and then thought better of it, opening the door again—Assu was a drinker, and if he had any alcohol in the car I'd need it later. I opened the glove compartment and found a bottle of cheap grain alcohol—and a wad of twenty-dollar bills. I stared at them, trying to decide if it would be safe to take them. Would they be traceable? Probably not. Could I risk it? I stared a moment longer, then shoved the money into one pocket of my pants and the bottle into another. I wiped everything down again, closed the door and locked it, then wiped down the outside handles as well. Two blocks later I dropped the keys into a sewer grate.

Assu, I was pretty sure, had killed himself on purpose. I should have seen it coming, after all the nihilistic talk about loss and endings at the bar. But I'd been so focused on what I wanted, and the things I needed to know, that I hadn't thought about what he wanted. Sociopathy will get you every time. He'd given up on life, right in front of my eyes, and I hadn't even seen it.

He couldn't feel cold, but he generated heat. The Withered worked in trade-offs, so that's probably how this worked as well: anytime he got cold, his body would heat up higher and higher, until he had to let that heat out somehow. Sometimes he did it by burning people, like he had with Luke Minaker, and sometimes he burned other things, or even melted them, like that glass in the bar. And then he'd locked himself in a fridge, and his body had built up so much heat trying to protect him from it, and he hadn't let it out at all, until it consumed him completely. He was done with the world, after too many years, so he left it.

Maybe it was Nobody, or someone he'd thought was Nobody. Talking to another Withered, maybe for the first time in decades—maybe centuries—had put him into a dark mood and pushed him over the edge.

It was about a mile walk back to the mortuary, and I managed to do it without any random farmers trying to drown me. I stopped about a block away, took a sip of the alcohol, and swished it around in my mouth before spitting it out; it burned my mouth, and almost made me gag, but I stayed in control and recapped the bottle. It was eleven o'clock at night, and it would be easy for Margo and the others to believe that the random stranger they'd just met yesterday had spent the whole evening out drinking somewhere. Better a drunk than a wanted arsonist.

A crowd of neighbors had gathered to watch the firefighters, though the fire was already out and didn't appear to have damaged much of the exterior. I found Margo and walked up to her, somewhat shakily, being sure to exhale near her face and let my breath be my excuse.

"Robert," she said, "thank goodness. When Harold couldn't find you in your room, we thought the worst."

"What happened?" I asked. I didn't slur my speech; that seemed a little much.

"Fire inside," said Margo. "Embalming room."

"Looks like arson," said Harold, "but they don't know who it was. One of the neighbors saw a red car speeding away."

Assu's car was green. Sometimes bad night vision was a criminal's best friend.

"That sucks," I said. I was too exhausted to sound intelligent, but that only helped sell my drunk excuse.

Margo took the bottle from my hand. "You're too young for this."

"You don't know how old I am."

"I know you're too young for this." She gave the bottle to Harold, who took it without a word and walked off through the crowd.

Had I cleaned up all the sludge? Even if I had, would that be enough? Agent Mills, the FBI agent who'd found me in Oklahoma, had said he'd been following me through arson cases. I'd been so careful since then, barely lighting any fires at all, and only when I could contain them, but I couldn't contain this. I'd hidden the soulstuff, and I'd hidden my own connection to it, but that still might not be enough.

I was always running, and always hiding.

I couldn't leave Lewisville, not with Rain and all her Withered right here just waiting to be found. But I had to leave the mortuary, no matter how much I loved it. I needed a new place to stay, and a new job, and I needed to do it without totally cutting my ties to Margo and the others, in case I ever needed to come back and ask them questions. It was the place I was most likely to be found, but it was still the best way to examine any future Withered victims. I needed to quit, but in a nice way, so they still liked me—

"Fire chief says it's just the one room," said Margo. "Bit of hallway, bit of crawl space in the attic. We can go back to work tomorrow."

"I need to—"

"We're getting Luke Minaker in two days," said Margo. "Fridge is shot, but we've still got the old one, and I need your help hauling it out of storage to see if it works. And then I need everything you've got on the makeup, because he was burned pretty bad."

"Okay," I said. The FBI wouldn't show up that fast. I could embalm one body. It had been so long.

I hadn't counted the money in my pocket yet, but it couldn't be too much. Not enough for an apartment, or even an extended-stay hotel. What I did have was a local junior college, and that meant apartments full of junior college students. Many of them would be upstanding citizens, but some would be directionless and unmotivated, living on their own for the first time without any of the skills to do it right. Exactly the kind of people who might let a random stranger—even a drunk—crash on their couch for a few weeks. I just had to meet them. Which meant I needed an aimless, screw-up college-age friend to introduce me.

Margo's last charity case.

Jasmyn.

CHAPTER 7

"Okay," I said, staring at the old refrigeration unit. "Are you ready for this?"

Jasmyn scoffed. "I realize that I am a strong and liberated woman, but yes, I can still wash something."

"It's not the washing," I said, picking up a face mask. "It's the smelling. You ever cleaned out an old fridge?"

"Not cleaned," she said. "But I've opened one that had been turned off for a couple of months. It was like every leftover the fridge had ever held was coming back to life and punching me in the face."

"Exactly," I said. "And this fridge's leftovers were all dead bodies."

"Awesome," said Jasmyn, snarling at the fridge and grabbing a face mask of her own. "Bring it."

"Here," I said, and held up a bottle of perfume I'd found on the shelf by the embalming fluids—a lot of morticians kept a good fragrance in the back room to help with the occasional corpse-y smell. I sprayed it in the air between us, waved my face mask through it, and then strapped it over my mouth and nose. She did the same. "Ready?"

"I'd say I was born for this," she said, "but that would be super depressing."

Margo's old refrigerator had spent several months in storage, ever since she'd upgraded to the new one Assu had destroyed. We'd wheeled it into the embalming room and plugged it in, hoping the cold would help deal with the smell by the time we were done washing all the dust off the outside. Now the outside was sparkling like a dream sequence, and we couldn't stall any longer. I opened the first door, and let the stench wash over us.

It wasn't filthy, just old. The unit had four chambers, two up and two down, so Jasmyn and I took opposite corners and started washing, doing our best to stay out of each other's way. We had a bucket full of hot, soapy water—only one bucket, because the other one was mysteriously missing—and a bottle full of industrial disinfectant. We also had rags, but we were dealing with long, narrow, body-shaped tunnels, so the only way to reach the back was with mops. I took the lower left chamber and tried not to grumble every time Jasmyn's mop dripped soapy corpse water on my head from her spot in the upper right.

I waited for her to make conversation, but she didn't. I needed to become her friend so I could find a new place to stay, and that meant conversation. Looked like I had to start it myself. I braced myself mentally and dove in.

"So I've been in Lewisville three days now," I said. "It's kind of . . ." I didn't know how to finish that sentence without sounding fake or insulting.

"Boring?" she offered.

"You said it," I told her, "not me."

"It's kind of fun if you like hiking. We have lots of great trails and stuff out in the canyons."

I scraped the mop back and forth across the back of the chamber. "You go hiking a lot?"

"No, I hate it," she said. "But I mean, I *hear* we have good trails. If you're into that."

"Lewisville must be worse than I thought," I said. "Your go-to defense of your town is a thing you don't even like to do? This place must be terrible."

She groaned. "You have no idea. It's not really that bad, though. But I don't know why I'm defending it because it's not really my town, anyway. I've only been here a year."

"Where'd you move from?" I asked. "Down by the border?"

"Border?" She stopped scrubbing and looked at me. "You think I'm Mexican."

I frowned. "You're not?"

"Not even close," she said, and pumped her fist in the air. "Yes! Another racist detected by the awesome super-powers of Jasmyn Shahi."

"We're in Arizona," I said. "Is it racist to assume the Latina girl is Mexican?"

"I'm not even Latina," she said, and made a loud explosion noise with her mouth. "He is powerless before my might."

"I'm sorry," I said. "My hometown is kind of overwhelmingly white, so I don't have a lot experience identifying the other options. Can I ask where you're from, then?"

"Ohio."

"I mean ethnically."

"I know," she said. "I'm just being difficult at this point."

"I bet you get the Mexican thing all the time, right?"

"You have no idea," she said, gritting her teeth as she scrubbed with her mop. "But honestly, I don't really mind. As patriotic as some of these people are, I'd probably get a lot more crap from them if they knew what I really was."

"Which is?"

"Persian," she said. "First generation Iranian-American. But this way I have a whole Latino support system instead of being the one lone Persian girl."

"I hadn't thought of that." I wrung out my mop in the bucket, then started scrubbing again. "So why'd you move from Ohio?"

"Because I *thought* I liked hiking," she said. "And I thought I liked accounting, and Lewis College has a good accounting program, so why not move down here and kill two birds with one stone? But then it turned out I hated both things, so all I had was two dead birds and nowhere to go. So I came here to the mortuary and got a job with Margo."

"Drawn in by the siren song of dead-body smell," I said.

"It's my favorite."

"Seriously, though, what *did* bring you here?" I asked. "I was born into mortuary life, and Harold too, and Margo married into it. You're the only one who's here by choice."

"Hand me the disinfectant," she said. I handed it up, and she sprayed a few more blasts into the refrigeration chamber. "I don't know if I'm here by choice," she said. "I mean, I chose it, but it's not like I had a lot of other choices clamoring for my attention. Margo came to me, and I didn't have anything else to do, so I did this."

I set down my mop and started scrubbing at the mouth of the chamber with my rag. "Margo just . . . came to you? Out of nowhere?"

"We met at a funeral," said Jasmyn.

"Makes sense." I gave the chamber a final wipe and started working on the door. We worked in silence for a moment, while I desperately tried to think of something to say. And then Jasmyn said it first:

"You're not asking me the obvious question."

I stopped, trying to think of what I'd missed. "Whose funeral?"

"Okay," she said, "I mean the other obvious question."

"You're not going to tell me who died?"

"Some kid from school." She used her rag to pick out grime from around the edge of her door's rubber seal. "What you're not asking me is why I didn't go home."

She was right. She'd come from Ohio for college, and when that didn't work out she could have gone back. Her family was there. I stared at the fridge a long time before answering. "That kind of thing doesn't really occur to me," I said. "I can't exactly go home either."

"I'm sorry."

"So why didn't you go home?"

"I don't like talking about it."

I laughed. "Then why did you bring it up?"

"Because everyone brings it up," she said. "I was just trying to get ahead of it, so you'd know not to ask."

"That didn't work very well."

"Do you want to get dinner tonight?" she asked suddenly. Her voice sped up. "There's actually like a group of us getting together at this place that does Mexican pizza, it's like a whole thing here in Lewisville—they put maraschino cherries on the Hawaiian ones for some reason—and it's kind of an informal thing, but I thought since you don't know anybody it'd be nice to get to . . . know some more people. If you're interested."

I do this all the time: I take something totally normal,

like getting to know someone, and turn it into a meticulous plan, like I'm going to rob a casino. I don't need to
manipulate people, because people aren't like me. I just
need to ask, and they'll say yes, because friendship is a normal thing that normal people do every day.

"That sounds good," I said. "Assuming that Mexican
pizza includes vegetarian options—I'm one of *those* people."

"I think they have a nopal one."

"What's nopal?"

"Cactus."

"Perfect," I said. "My doctor keeps telling me I need
more cactus."

"It's actually pretty good," said Jasmyn. "Though again,
like with hiking, I'm mostly just repeating what I've heard
other people say."

"Cool," I said. "What time?"

"Um . . . dinnertime? I don't know. I'll tell you once I
get a chance to check my phone. Now I have another
question."

I took a breath, not knowing what to expect.

"Are you ready to switch?" asked Jasmyn. "I think this
cadaver tube's about as clean as I'm going to get it."

The restaurant was called Nacho Parrot, which more or
less told you everything you needed to know about it. The
customers were mostly early twentysomethings from the

junior college, the menu was "edgy," in that it contained a lot of comic-book fonts, and the food was almost hilariously proud of how hip it was. I stepped up to the register and ordered the Rico Suave, which was mostly cactus and goat cheese and Hatch green chilies, and then paid with Assu's money. Jasmyn introduced me to her friends while we waited at our booth.

"This is Nate," she said first, pointing to a lanky, vaguely bearded man in a shapeless hat. "He's majoring in . . . visual art? Visual design?"

"Visual communication," said Nate. "It's basically illustration."

"I didn't realize Lewis College had an illustration program," I said.

"They don't," said Nate. "It's called visual communication. It's like half illustration and half marketing."

"Cool." I didn't know anything about any of those subjects, and I worried that I'd offended him by my attempt at small talk, so I determined to keep quieter until I knew the group dynamic a little better.

"This is Al!sha," said Jasmyn. "She's in theater, so she spells it with an exclamation mark instead of an 'i.'"

"And it's so annoying," said Nate.

"No theater anymore," said Al!sha, "I'm back in technical writing again. So if you need someone bitter and underpaid to describe a simple process in agonizing detail, I'm your woman."

"You hated technical writing," said Jasmyn. "Why'd you go back?"

"Because my dad won't pay for anything else," said Al!sha.

"Hey guys," said another boy. He walked to the table holding hands with a girl. Both were wearing glasses with thick black frames. "I brought my girlfriend, I hope that's cool."

"Jazz brought her boyfriend," said Nate.

"He's not my boyfriend," said Jasmyn. "We just work together, and he's new in town."

"Hey," said the boy, and reached out his hand to shake mine. "I'm Parker."

Nate grinned. "Which is both his name and his job."

"Shut up," said Parker, smacking him and pushing him further into the booth. He kept pushing him until there was room for both himself and his girlfriend. "Everyone, this is Shelby. Shelby, this is everyone: Nate, Jazz, Al!sha with an exclamation point, and new guy."

"Robert," said Jasmyn.

"He can introduce himself," said Nate.

"What," said Jasmyn, "and Shelby can't? You don't complain when a woman doesn't get to speak for herself, but heaven forbid a man sits there and lets a girl take the lead."

"Girl*friend*," said Al!sha.

"She's not my girlfriend," I said. "I've known her for two days."

"Though we did clean out a corpse fridge together today," said Jasmyn, "so we're pretty close."

"So how do we order?" asked Shelby. "Is this, like, a slice-by-slice place, or do we all pitch in for a whole pizza?"

"Slice by slice," said Parker. "The menu's on the wall over there; pick something you like, and I'll go place the order."

"Adobada's the best," said Jasmyn.

"I've never had Mexican pizza," said Shelby, "so I'd probably better start with something I recognize. Do they have, like, a taco pizza?"

"Technically, any pizza you fold in half is a taco pizza," said Jasmyn.

"Taco isn't a food," said Nate, "it's a food category, defined by a delivery system. That's like asking for a sandwich pizza without specifying the sandwich type—is it a club? A Reuben? A hamburger?"

"A hamburger is not a sandwich," said Al!sha, "it's a burger."

"Ignore them," said Parker to Shelby. "I don't even know why I spend time with them. They're terrible people."

"A hamburger is totally a sandwich," said Nate.

"A hamburger is not on par with 'club' and 'Reuben' as sandwich types," said Al!sha. "It's a category, just like sandwich—but it's not *a* sandwich."

Jasmyn smiled at me. "Aren't you glad you came?"

"It's two pieces of bread and something in between

them," said Nate. "Any rational human being would classify it as a—"

"What about a Big Mac?" asked Jasmyn. "They have three pieces of bread." She held up her hand to Al!sha, who high-fived it without even looking.

"Wait," said Parker. "That definition of sandwich would include not just hamburgers but hot dogs, which is patently ridiculous."

"A hot dog is totally a sandwich," said Nate.

"If anything," said Jasmyn, "a hot dog is a taco, because the two pieces of bun are connected." She drew a giant circle in the air. "And now we're back to the beginning, and I just blew your minds."

I looked at Shelby. "I hope that helped answer your question about the menu."

"Close enough," Shelby said, and pointed at Nate. "I want the first thing he said—a Reuben pizza."

Everyone stared at her.

"No," said Parker, "this is all just Mexican food."

Shelby smirked. "Then why did he say there was a Reuben pizza?"

"Just ignore him," said Parker, "he's an idiot."

"Order the carne asada," said Al!sha. "It's the best."

"Adobada's the best," said Jasmyn. "Trust me."

"Carne asada's fine," Shelby said, and looked at Jasmyn. "I'm sure your one is delicious, though."

"I'll give you a bite," said Jasmyn. "You'll see."

"So what's the news?" asked Parker. "Anything big?"

I accidentally helped an ancient sun god immolate himself in a refrigerator, I thought, but I didn't say it out loud.

"Al!sha-with-an-exclamation-point switched back to technical writing," said Nate. "Again."

"Again?" asked Parker. "I thought you were theater for sure this time."

"My dad won't pay for theater," said Al!sha. "And honestly I don't even care—I'm better off. Have you ever ridden in a car with a group of theater people? It doesn't matter what song comes on, everyone sings along with the harmony line. No melody."

"I have to assume, though," said Nate, "that you get a lot less nudity in tech writing."

"We know," said Parker, "we know: you're in illustration, and you work with live nude models. Give it a rest."

"It's called visual communication," said Nate.

"None of my theater work was nude," said Al!sha. "That sex scene was entirely behind a screen—you guys would know that if you'd ever come to see it."

"Wait," said Shelby, "I think I saw that. Was it last fall, in the Twitchell Theater?"

"That's the one!" said Al!sha. "That's amazing, I thought nobody saw that one!"

"My boyfriend at the time was in it—Scott Kraczek?"

"He's the one I had fake sex with!" Al!sha said, and then crinkled her nose. "He was such an a-hole, though."

"He was," said Shelby. "Total a-hole."

"You can just say the real word," said Nate. "We're not going to melt in its presence."

"Excuse me for a minute," said Jasmyn, standing up, "I need to go outside for some air. Let me know when the pizza gets here." She walked to the door.

"So maybe Jazz would melt in its presence," said Nate, "but the rest of us are fine."

"Is she okay?" asked Shelby. "She looked really bothered by something."

"She just does this sometimes," said Parker. "She'll be back. And we still need to order—you want carne asada?"

"Yes, please," said Shelby.

"Be right back." They shared a quick kiss. "Finish talking about the ex-boyfriend before I get back, okay? I'm amazing, but not amazing enough to want to listen to that." He went to stand in line at the counter, and Shelby and Al!sha turned back to each other, gossiping about the ex. Nate turned to me.

"So," he said. "I think you've said six entire words since you got here. What's your deal?"

"I'm quiet," I said.

"I don't mean why aren't you talking," he said. "Obviously you're quiet, that's a given. But who are you, where are you from, why do you work with dead bodies? All that kind of stuff."

"My name's Robert," I said. I didn't want to sleep on Nate's couch if I could avoid it, but if this is what it took to hide from the FBI, I could make peace with anyone. Or at least I could try. "I'm from a little town you've probably never heard of called Fetridge, Nebraska." I'd seen it on a sign once. "I work with dead bodies because my parents were morticians, and I just kind of grew up with it."

"That's gross," said Nate.

"Only if you treat it grossly," I said.

"It's also very matter-of-fact," said Nate. " 'Here's what I do, here's where I'm from: *X, Y, Z*, all in a row.' What do you *like*? What do you *do*? Who *are* you?"

I really didn't like this guy. "Those are deep questions."

"I'm an artist," he said. "This is how we are."

I managed to stop myself from rolling my eyes. "An artist and a marketer," I said. "How can I resist the double threat?"

"By giving in and answering."

I shrugged. I wasn't really prepared to talk about myself, especially considering that the only self I could talk about was a fake alias I would be making up on the spot. "Well," I said. "I like . . ." There were only a handful of people I knew well enough to describe on the spot, and only one of them was a mortician. So I described my mom. "I like eighties music. And cooking—like, not just 'making dinner' kind of cooking, but 'experimenting with fancy recipes' kind of cooking. The kind that's almost like chemistry. And I don't watch a lot of TV, but when I do it's lawyer shows or the news. And I like . . ." I could feel my memories shifting as I spoke, buried ideas churning up to the surface as I struggled to define her in some kind of understandable way. "My job. My family, back when I had one. And I never really . . . had time for them, all the time? Not because I ignored them but because I had a lot to do, and I had to juggle it all, and I had to make it work. And I don't know if they understood that at the time, but they do now. I mean, I think they do—I hope they do."

Nate looked uncomfortable. "This isn't really what I meant for you to talk about."

"But it's what you asked," I said. "And this is the answer. You asked who I was, and who people are is never simple. I don't think I ever understood my family or myself or anyone, and I probably still don't, and I guarantee that you don't, and it's because we don't want to look at the bad stuff."

"I know this goes against the point you're trying to make," said Al!sha, "but you just described Nate more accurately than I have ever heard anyone describe him." I didn't even realize she was listening.

"Fonda Rodolfo," said a waiter, holding a tray full of pizza slices. Nate raised his hand, and the waiter set a plate in front of him. "Caballo Cebolla?" Al!sha. "Rico Suave?" Me. "Chupacadobada?"

"That's Jasmyn's," said Nate.

"Parker's not even back yet," said Shelby.

"I'll go get her," I said, and slid out of the booth. I walked outside and breathed deep. The sky was still bright and hot, with wavy lines of heat mirage floating up from the scorching asphalt of the parking lot. But it was real in a way that the air-conditioned restaurant wasn't, and I closed my eyes and reveled in the slow, warm eddies buried within the harsh, oppressive air.

I was more shaken by my conversation with Nate than I should have been. Or I guess more shaken than I wanted to be.

Jasmyn was leaning her forearms on a metal parking barrier by the side of the brick building, perched against the wall in a slim sliver of shade. She seemed lost in her thoughts, and I took a moment to clear my own before walking over to her. I hesitated in the fringes of her peripheral vision, trying to phrase the summons to dinner in way that was friendly or charming or at least not stupid. But after a moment I shook my head and slipped into the shade next to her and leaned on the same bar. It had once been painted red, but most of the paint had flaked off.

"I needed some air, too," I said.

"That group can be . . . a lot," she said.

"Food's here."

"Cool."

Neither of us moved. Cars sped past on the road; the tar in the cracks had grown soft in the heat and smeared in long lines as the tires ran over it.

"I lied to you this morning," said Jasmyn.

I shrugged. "Most people do."

"I didn't meet Margo at a funeral." She paused, and I

waited. "I met her at a support group." She paused again. "For rape survivors."

She had left the restaurant when Al!sha was talking about sex. Pieces clicked together in my head.

She didn't want to go back to Ohio.

"I don't like talking about it," she said. "Obviously. But I need to. And it's more . . . I don't know. It's easier when I'm talking to people who know what it's like. And I think you do."

"I don't know exactly," I said, and paused. "But I guess I can guess. I don't know rape but I know . . . trauma."

"I thought so," she said.

We watched the road, and I counted the cars in my head and wondered where they were going, and why, and if they even wanted to go there or if they were just swept along by the road itself, like a river. Roads don't flow with water, they flow with momentum; once you get on one, it's hard to get off.

"My mother killed herself," I said. I don't know why I said it—I guess describing Mom to Nate had put me in a different state of mind. "It wasn't a normal suicide, like she hated her life or whatever. Someone attacked us, and they were trying to kill me, and she killed herself to save me."

"So she sacrificed herself," said Jasmyn. "That's different than killing herself."

I picked at the flecks of paint still clinging to the old metal bar. "It's complicated."

Another car drove by, the tires thudding across the cracks and spreading the tar just a tiny bit farther.

"Do you hate him?" she asked. "The man who attacked you?"

"Yes." It wasn't a man, it was Nobody. Whom I'd lived with for over a year since the attack, and gotten to know, and even pretended to be. "And no. I guess that's complicated, too."

"It always is," said Jasmyn.

I thought about Nobody, and Assu, and Elijah, and Crowley and all the others I'd met, and all the things they'd given up just to be who they'd become. To survive. Assu had said it was fun in the beginning, but that by the end it was just survival—momentum carrying him forward until he couldn't do anything else. And then "anything else" turned out to be suicide.

Had Assu started like this, like I was right now? Leaning on a fence somewhere, talking about his trauma, trying to find some way to get past it? He hadn't set out to become a monster: Rain had given him the chance to give his pain away, and he'd done it. He wasn't just ending at survival, he'd started there. All of them had.

"Would you give it up?" I asked Jasmyn. "If you could . . . lose your rape, like literally take it out of your life so it had never happened, would you do it?"

Jasmyn thought for a moment, but shook her head. "No."

"Why not?"

"Because it's a part of who I am now. If it had never happened, I wouldn't be me. I'd be a version of me who'd never been attacked—and never hated herself, and never OD'd on sleeping pills, and never ran away from home. And never healed. And maybe that version of me would be happier, or simpler, or something, but she wouldn't be *better*. She wouldn't be *worth* any more than I am now. It took a long time for me to love myself, but now I do, so why would I give that self away?" She flicked a piece of peeled red paint into the parking lot. "That's what they tell us in the support group: that everybody's worth saving. Even me." She scratched another flake of paint with her fingernail. "Even him."

"Do you believe it?"

Another fleck of paint. "No," she said at last. "But I'm trying to."

"Yo, lovebirds," said Parker. We turned, and saw him hanging out of the front door of the restaurant. "Your disgusting vegetarian pizza's getting cold."

"Let's go," said Jasmyn.

"Hey Parker," I said, straightening up. I needed to do what Jasmyn had done that morning and just come right out and ask my question. "I'm kind of creeped out living in the mortuary, do you have a couch I could crash on for a week or two?"

"Sure," said Parker. "Just no drugs, okay? My landlord already hates me."

CHAPTER 8

The mortuary had two main entrances, plus the garage and the receiving door where the bodies came and went in hearses and coroner transport vehicles. Plus my room, which technically wasn't my room anymore, so I couldn't control the door. That meant five entrances I had to watch if I was going to spend any more time in the funeral home. If an agent of the FBI came to one of them, I needed to know about it, and I needed time to escape out one of the other ones.

My old room was the easiest. As long as Margo didn't rent it out to anyone, it would stay locked and empty. I worried that maybe someone would open it casually, trying to get a breeze or something, but this was an Arizona summer: everything was sealed shut tighter than a space station, and the air conditioning ran full blast. Just to be sure, during my lunch break the next day, I loosened the screws in the door latch, making it stick when someone tried to open it. So that was one door taken care of.

The others were harder. The mortuary didn't have any security cameras, as I'd learned when I first considered breaking in, but they did have a motion sensor connected to an alarm, which in turn connected to an antitheft call center somewhere. Could I mess with that at all? Probably not, without alerting the call center that something was up. Preventing people from tampering with their equipment was practically their whole job. I'd need something else. The ideal solution, of course, was some kind of camera system, so I could know when someone was coming and then immediately see if they were a threat. That was probably out of my price range.

The burnt corpse of Luke Minaker never showed up—the autopsy was more problematic than they were expecting—so I went to the hardware store after work and looked for motion-sensing lights, like the kind you'd put in your driveway. Most of them were around seventy or eighty bucks apiece, but I found a cheap-looking brand on sale for sixty. The roll of bills I'd taken from Assu's car contained $200, minus the $4.95 I'd spent on Mexican pizza, and with my own meager savings, I managed to raise my grand total to $286.18. Four lights was $240.

I put them in my cart and went to the doorbell section, but the cheapest wireless doorbell I could find was thirty dollars—that was way beyond my limit. I looked again, wondering if I'd missed something, but I couldn't find anything cheaper.

I flagged down one of the sales people. "Do you have any cheaper doorbells? The wireless ones?"

"Not in the store, but we do have some online."

"I need to buy them today," I said, "is there any way you could give me the online price?"

"It's not an item we carry here, just at the central ware-house. You have to order online."

"Okay," I said. "How about these driveway lights?"

"I'm afraid that if you want the motion sensor, what you've got in the cart is already the best we can do."

"But I need something cheaper. Is there any way you can make me a deal?"

"You're buying motion sensors and wireless receivers," the man said. "That's the most expensive option in both categories. Is there a way you could alter your project with a standard light fixture, or maybe a standard doorbell?"

If only he knew what my project was. "No, it's got to be these."

"Four sets of each. Is this for an apartment complex?"

"Exactly," I said. "I'll let my boss know this is the best I can do. Thanks."

"No problem. Let me know if you need anything else." He smiled and walked away, and I stared at my cart full of boxes. I could afford three sets. Which door of the mortuary could I risk not watching? None of them. Maybe I could shoplift the fourth set? I looked around, wondering where the cameras were, but decided that it was too risky regardless. Shoplifting was not on my resume, and three sets was better than nothing. I put the fourth one back, paid at the register, and spent another twenty bucks on batteries. I walked home with the bag over my shoulder and my other hand up under my T-shirt, clutched tight around the handle of a small steak knife I'd borrowed from Parker's kitchen. No one followed me or tried to drown me. I got back to Parker's place, returned the knife to its drawer, and dumped out my boxes on the floor. He wouldn't be back from his date for another few hours, so I had time to work unimpeded.

A motion-sensor light was really two devices: a motion sensor and a light. When the former detected movement in its field of view, it sent a signal along a little wire and turned on the latter. The doorbells were the same: push the button and a signal goes through a wire to a little wireless beacon, which sent another signal through the air to a chime box. All I had to do was get the trigger from the first one to talk to the second one. I opened the packages, pried apart the devices, and basically just fiddled around with wires and knives and screwdrivers until I somehow made it work. Trigger the motion sensor, and it rang the doorbell. I rigged the other two sensors to work the same way, loaded them up with fresh new batteries, and stashed them in my backpack. I took the lights and all the rest of the parts and packaging outside to the communal Dumpster and threw it all in. When Parker came home I was already lying on the couch, pretending to be asleep.

The next morning I got to work early and walked all around the building, trying to decide which door least needed an alarm. Obviously the front door needed one; I placed a motion sensor in the garden nearby, aimed it at the walkway, and used rocks to hide it and secure it in place. I turned it on, walked up the door, and the chime box in my backpack rang out a classic *ding-dong*. I went around to the back and did the same, covering the rear door people would use if they approached from the parking lot. I tested it, and the second chime box made the same *ding-dong* sound. It was great that they both worked, but if one of them rang and I had seconds to get away, I'd need to know which door someone had used. They claimed to have sixteen different tones, so I opened the chime box and puzzled for a minute over which settings to use. Most of them were just variations of the same basic tones, and I needed something instantly recognizable. "Auld Lang Syne"? Beethoven's Fifth? I set the back door to "Happy Birthday," and the final chime to "We Wish You A Merry Christmas." The front could stay as it was.

But which of the last two doors should I alarm? The garage door and the receiving door were far enough apart that I didn't think I could cover them both with a single sensor. I hemmed and hawed for a bit, trying to work out the best of two bad choices, and settled on the receiving door: it went practically straight into the embalming room, which is where I'd spend most of my time, so if anyone came to that I needed to know ASAP. I put the alarm at the base of a bush, tucked in just under the leaves, and angled it to catch both the door and as much of the path leading up to it as I could. I tested it, and the chime box in my backpack sang a cheerful Christmas carol. It worked.

Barely half a second later my backpack sang again: *ding-dong.* Someone was coming in the front door, probably Margo. I anchored the last sensor with a couple more rocks and zipped my backpack closed. I counted to twenty and walked around to the front. My backpack ding-donged again as I went in.

Margo was in her office. "Good morning, Robert."

"Morning."

"We're getting the Minaker body today. You ready?"

"Disturbingly ready," I said. Margo raised her eyebrow, and I smiled. "I'll go prep the room."

The body of Lucas Minaker arrived at 10 A.M., and we laid him out on the table and unzipped the body bag. Jasmyn grimaced and looked away. He was burned from head to toe, hairless and earless and in many places skinless; what skin was left was scorched in an intricate, semi-random pattern of yellow and brown and black, stretched tight over his bones and well-cooked muscles. He looked like a bratwurst.

"Give yourself a minute," said Margo. "Your first burn-body is always hard."

Jasmyn sat down, breathing shallowly, and Margo gently pushed the girl's head down toward her knees. I started as we always started, by examining the body in careful detail, making sure nothing was wrong or out of the ordinary before we got to work. The first part of this process was, technically, making sure the body was dead, but in this case it was obvious—not only was it burned, but the autopsy had opened his chest in a giant *Y*-shaped cut: shoulder to sternum, shoulder to sternum, and sternum to waist. They had cracked his ribs and opened him up like a suitcase, removing the internal organs and examining them, and then putting them in a plastic bag and storing them back in the chest cavity. I could see a corner of this bag poking out of the gap in the *Y* incision.

"Been a while since we had an autopsy," said Margo. "Kathy didn't get one."

"Most people don't," I said. "Surprising she didn't, though. Didn't anyone suspect foul play?"

"You'd think," said Margo. "Just an accident, though. Drinking a glass of water or something."

At home, in my mom's mortuary, her twin sister Margaret would have called organs by now—an autopsy embalming was done in two parts: one for the circulatory system and one for the removed organs. The latter was easier. "Jasmyn," I said. "Have you done an organ embalming?"

"Yes."

"Then take these," I said, opening the chest and pulling out the bag. "We'll set you up on the other table, and you can face away from us and just deal with these. The heat that burned him didn't get this deep, so they're pretty much just normal organs. It'll be simple and familiar."

"I can do the body." She took a deep breath, long and slow and controlled, and then stood up. After a moment she raised her eyes and looked at the burned body. "I can do this."

"Just do the organs," said Margo.

"Don't coddle me," said Jasmyn.

"It's not coddling, it's business," said Margo. "I know *you* can do an arterial embalm, now I want to see how the new guy handles it."

"Fine," said Jasmyn. She hadn't taken her eyes off the body yet. She stared a moment longer, her teeth clenched, and then turned away abruptly to the other table. Like she'd been holding her breath underwater and now it was time to pull out. I gave her the bag and she got to work, carefully mixing an embalming formula of germicide, anticoagulant, perfume, and glutaraldehyde—a knockoff of formaldehyde that a lot of mortuaries were using these days. It wasn't as toxic, but it wasn't as effective, either. Normally you'd mix a dye in there as well, but the organs didn't need that. I thought about the poison chemicals and looked up at the ceiling, where our old embalming room had had a big metal ventilator hood to suck out the fumes.

"Let's hope this fan doesn't give out on us," I said.

"There's four of them and they're brand new," said Margo. "Had them put in last winter."

"Just a thing I like to say," I said. That had been my aunt Margaret's thing, too.

The inside of the body wasn't as cooked as the outside, and the blood vessels were still in pretty good condition. We'd be able to do a full arterial embalming, but first we had to finish the inspection. I zipped the body bag the rest of the way down, exposing his lower half—his groin area was horrifying—and Margo and I pulled the now-empty bag out from under him. Moving the bag exposed his arms, and Margo and I stared at them in surprise.

His forearms had one spot each, perfectly hand-shaped, with no burned flesh whatsoever.

"Well," said Margo. "You don't see that every day."

"Thank goodness," I said.

I touched one of the unburned patches, prodding it with my finger. It was soft and almost mushy, like dead bodies were supposed to be, without any of the firmness of the parts that were more cooked. I picked up the arm and rotated it gently, looking at the handprint—it was unmistakably a hand. I wanted to test it for size against the marks on my backpack, but there was no way to do that without making Margo and Jasmyn curious about questions I really didn't want to answer; I'd pinned a T-shirt over my backpack to cover the handprints, and thus far I'd managed to hide them and the entire attack from everyone. Instead I put my own hand on the print, test-ing it for size that way, hoping I could draw a useful com-parison to the backpack prints later. I was surprised to find that my hand only fit the print on the arm when the arm was flat against the body's sides, as if Assu had just walked up in front of him and grabbed Lucas's arms. I had ex-pected the opposite, with the grip reversed, as if Lucas's arms had been raised in front of his face in a defensive position. What did it mean?

And what did it matter, if the Withered who'd done it was already dead? Could I learn anything from the body that would help me find the others? Or was it all just mor-bid fascination?

My backpack chirped a cheerful "We Wish You A Merry Christmas," and I grabbed it and bolted for the door.

"Cell phone," I said, "I gotta take this." That song meant someone was at the receiving door, and I didn't have any time to spare. I got into the hall, slung my back-pack over my shoulders, and got ready to bolt. First I had to see who it was, though, so I lurked outside of the em-balming room and listened.

The sound of a door in the adjoining room. Footsteps. "Margo, you here?" I thought I recognized the man's voice, but I couldn't place it. Not Harold. Younger.

"Come on in, Simon," called Margo. More footsteps. "You brought me that new shipment of detergents?"

"Right here," said the man. More footsteps. "Hey Jazz—*good night*, why didn't you warn me?"

"It's a dead body," said Jasmyn. "What did you expect to see in an embalming room?"

More footsteps and the heavy *thunk* of a box being set down on a counter. "I'm gonna start leaving these damn boxes on the sidewalk if you keep scaring me like this."

They made idle small talk while Margo signed for the package, and I wondered: if he was just a delivery man, then I was safe, wasn't I? He wasn't from the FBI. But I'd heard his voice somewhere before, and that made me nervous. It wasn't any of Jasmyn's friends, and I didn't know anybody else in the city. What if it was someone who knew me from another city, under a different name? I couldn't risk being seen. I walked away quietly, moving toward one of the side rooms. There was a window there with a perfect view of the receiving door. I reached it just in time to peer out through a gap in the curtain and watched the man walk out into the sun and back to his truck. My backpack sang its Christmas song as he went.

He wasn't wearing the coat this time, but I knew him plain as day. He was the man who'd tried to drown me.

Should I follow him? Could I, even if I wanted to? I peered at the truck, trying to make out the license plate, but all I could see was the company logo on the side: DIAMOND DELIVERY. He got in and drove away.

Margo had called him by his first name: Alvin? Simon. If she was on a first-name basis, she'd know more about him as well. I could get all the info from her. I walked back to the embalming room, set my backpack in the corner, and washed up again.

"I heard you talking," I said.

"We didn't hear you," said Margo.

"I'm pretty quiet on the phone," I said. I nodded at the box of corpse detergent. "Delivery guy?"

"Panhandler," said Margo. "Now help me set these features before another one shows up."

"Yes, it was a delivery guy," said Jasmyn. "Margo, you're as bad as my friends from school."

"I'm sorry I missed him," I said. "Her friends from school are the only people I even know in this town."

"Lord have mercy on your soul," said Margo. "You're going to start spelling your name with a smiley face instead of an O."

"No way Robert uses a smiley face," said Jasmyn. "Maybe a devil emoji, though."

I said nothing, and got back to work.

Over the course of the afternoon I managed to deduce the delivery man's full name: Simon Jacob Watts. The motion sensors pinged one other time, but it was only Harold. When we finished embalming Minaker, I washed up, changed my clothes, and walked the three miles to the library, where I used their free Internet to find everything I possibly could about Watts, including his home address.

There wasn't much on him. No history of violence, no criminal record. I found an online map and wrote down the directions to his house, out in the suburbs. I zoomed in on the satellite image and stared at it, feeling like a missile drone looking down on my target. What would I do?

I walked out to find it, though it was another few miles from where I was. By the time I got there, it was already dark. A couple of windows were still bright, though I couldn't see anyone inside. The front lawn had a bike and a toddler-sized plastic car; apparently he had kids. I slipped around to the carport, being careful not to touch the car, in case he had an alarm. I peeked in the side windows and even opened the garbage can, though I didn't see anything immediately interesting. I slipped into the backyard and found that he had a small wooden deck outside his kitchen. It reminded me of the layout of Brooke's old house in Clayton. The kitchen light was on and the blinds were open, and I could see Simon and a woman I assumed was his wife sitting at the kitchen table, smiling and picking at leftovers. The clock on their wall said it was nearly ten in the evening, so I assumed the kids were asleep. Their fridge was covered with crayon drawings stuck up with magnets. A cat slept on the floor. I backed away, not wanting to attract its attention.

By every appearance, Simon Watts looked totally normal. But serial killers always did. He wasn't raving about the Dark Lady, or sharpening meat hooks, or cutting out letters from a magazine to write an anonymous note. He was just sitting there, talking to his wife, without a care in the world. And yet he was my only connection to Rain.

They didn't seem to have a dog, so I took the risk and looked for a place to hide. I found it in a plastic playhouse in their backyard. It was weathered by the sun and sported more than a few spider webs on the door; it didn't look like the kids used it very much. The night air was warm, and I didn't even need a blanket. I crept inside the playhouse, propped myself against the back wall, and sat with a perfect view of the back door and the car.

And settled down to watch him, all night long.

CHAPTER 9

Simon Watts didn't leave his house all night. And another drowned body was found in the morning.

I watched Watts get up and leave for work at about 6:30 A.M., and I slipped out of his backyard and walked to the mortuary. I was growing more and more familiar with the city the more I walked around in it, and especially after I got lost in a subdivision, but now I knew how that subdivision worked, and I guess that was useful information. Probably not, but I'd spent the night in a plastic playhouse, and Arizona nights were far colder than I'd been expecting, and I was trying to look on the bright side. I found my way out and arrived at the mortuary early, checked all the batteries in my motion sensors, and sat in the back and waited for Margo. She came in around eight. When I heard the chime from my backpack I walked back up to the front door. She gave me the news before she even said hello.

"Crabtree Jones drowned last night," she said. "Shelley found him on the property around three in the morning, out in the yard by the trucks. Apparently he never came back in to bed, and she woke up and wondered where he was and went looking for him."

A hundred questions leapt into my mind: how had someone drowned if Simon Watts hadn't done it? Where had it happened, and was it close to water? Did Rain have more than one visionary killer to do her bidding? These and more tumbled through my head, but after hunting Withered for so many years, I'd grown pretty good at hiding my investigations. The only question I asked out loud was this:

"There's a person named Crabtree Jones?"

"It's not his real name," said Margo, pulling some blank paperwork out of her desk. "I think it's Matthew, but nobody likes him and he owns the Crabtree Junkyard, so we all call him Crabtree. I say 'we' like I had some part in it, but they were all calling him Crabtree before I ever moved to Lewisville, back when his father owned the junkyard and he just lived there."

"Wait," I said. "There's a person named Crabtree Jones, and *he lives in a junkyard*?"

"Well where else is he supposed to live? You own a junkyard, you don't own much else. Crabtree's yard is on the highway, maybe ten, twelve miles outside of town. He buys old vehicles and strips them for parts. Or at least he used to, before he drowned."

I sat in the other office chair, watching as she started filling out the paperwork. "So how do you know all this?" I asked. "If his wife found him at 3 A.M., we don't exactly have a bustling local journalist scene to pick up on the story and get it out this early in the morning."

"Shelley called me."

"Why?"

"She's a friend of mine," said Margo, licking her finger and turning a page. "One of the blue-hairs that was here the other day for Kathy's viewing. You met her, though I can't imagine you remember. All us old ladies know each other. We have a secret club—handshakes and everything."

"Little Orphan Annie decoder rings," I suggested.

"That's the idea." She filled in a few more blanks on the paperwork, writing the date in careful, block lettering. "Shelley called me first thing in the morning, wants my help setting up the funeral."

I was curious and worn too thin to care about niceties, so I asked: "How old are you?"

Margo looked up. "Now what kind of question is that to ask a lady?"

"The women at the viewing were all seventy-five at

least, and Kathy looked mid-sixties. You keep putting yourself in the same group, but you don't look a day over . . ." I tried to guess, ". . . fifty-five."

"Don't lowball me, son. I earned these years."

"Sixty, then," I said. "But that's pushing it."

She finished the paperwork and stacked it neatly, lining up the edges of each page with fastidious attention to detail. "As it happens I'm a mite older than even that, but I'm not a blue-hair yet so you're right enough about the difference in our ages. For whatever that information is worth. Now, when are you gonna tell me why you look like you slept in a treehouse all night?"

One of the great things I've learned about my life is that it's weird enough that I can usually just tell the truth about it and no one will believe me. "It was a playhouse," I said. "Had a little plastic sink and everything. I'm working up to treehouses, but I'm afraid of heights."

"Well," said Margo. "You take your smart mouth into the shower and get washed up. We leave in ten minutes."

"Where are we going?"

"Have you not been listening? Crabtree died. You watched me fill out the paperwork for it."

"So, you're going out to the house to arrange the funeral?"

"I am a funeral director, after all. I don't know which part of this is so mysterious."

"My mom never made house calls."

Margo tucked the papers in a manila folder. "That's why you're coming with me. You want to be the kind of funeral director who gets a phone call at six in the morning from a newly minted widow, you make house calls." She stood up. "Nine minutes left for that shower."

I nodded and ran to the tiny locker room, showering in a flurry and then getting back into my dirty clothes because they were all I had with me. I brushed off the last bits of grass and dirt and ran out to meet Margo at her car.

"I suppose that'll have to do," she said. "Hop in."

Margo didn't talk much in the car, which gave me the chance to think more about the situation with the Withered. I knew there was at least one in town, and the continued occurrence of inexplicable drownings certainly hinted at another. I assumed it was Rain, because of what the homeless girl had said, but what if she'd meant something else? What if she was just high? I needed to find her and talk to her.

"Does Lewisville have a homeless shelter?" I asked.

"Not as such," said Margo. "Soup kitchens, though, and a halfway house." She glanced at me as she drove. "You can always move back into the mortuary."

"It's not for me," I said, "I'm just curious. Think maybe I'll volunteer."

"Good for you."

If the girl at the viewing had really been homeless, volunteering in that community might be the best way to find her or someone who knew her. And if a Withered was preying on local homeless, I might learn a bunch of other things as well.

In the meantime, what could I do about Simon Watts? He was obviously connected to something dangerous, and it seemed likely to me that the Dark Lady he'd talked about was a Withered, but I'd been wrong before. Could I risk just approaching him directly? Would he attack me when he saw me? Would he run? Would he even recognize me at all?

And now another man had drowned and there was no way Simon had done it. How many people did Rain have under her control? Was the homeless girl one of them? If I got too close, would the entire town rise up and attack me? I looked at Margo, wondering how I could kill her if she suddenly felt compelled to drown me. She was a large woman, solidly built, and probably pretty strong as well. I might be able to take her, but a knife would be easier. I needed to get my own again, instead of just borrowing Parker's all the time.

I needed to stop thinking about killing people. Or at least focus on killing the right people.

I wondered what Parker had thought when he'd realized I'd never come home the night before. Did he think I was a druggie? Probably most people did—a druggie or a drunk, but that was sometimes valuable. People made their own excuses for you, which saved a lot of time. And it was easier to maneuver around a person when you knew exactly what they thought of you.

We drove through a curving canyon of yellow and brown stone, dotted here and there with tenacious, twisted trees, and then the road straightened out into a wide, flat plain. I saw the junkyard a good five minutes before we reached it, an acre or two of fenced land stacked high with rusting cars. Margo exited the freeway, and then we turned sharp to the right and passed through a narrow tunnel underneath the road. The street was called Crabtree, and it was paved right up to the edge of the open gate of the Crabtree Junkyard. A wide sign hung over it, pale red letters faded by the sun. Inside the yard was a police car, parked by an old wooden house that looked so nice it seemed completely out of place.

Chalk body outlines are only used when the body is still alive, and they need to get it to the hospital before the police have finished studying a crime scene; they mark the body's location as best they can, and then medics try to save the person while the police stay behind and look at bullet angles and that kind of stuff. All of which is to say that there was no body outline here, just a yellow plastic card, folded in half, with a black number one on it, marking the place where the body had lain.

"Morning, Joe," said Margo, unfolding herself from behind the wheel of the car. "Brown's already taken him away?"

"Missed him by ten minutes at the most," said the cop.

"Blame him, then," said Margo, pointing at me. "Slept in a treehouse; needed a shower. I'm going in to talk to Shelley."

Margo walked toward the porch of the house, clutching her yellow folder tightly, but I stayed in the yard, trying to take it all in. The first thing to notice was the total lack of water: this was the full-blown Arizona desert, and with the sun already up, it was dry as a bone and climbing up toward scorching. The yellow card that marked the body's position was about ten yards out from the house, and another yard or so from the closest vehicle—an old, dusty truck, with more rust on it than paint.

The cop looked me up and down. "Another of Margo's charity cases?"

"Yep," I said, and walked toward him to shake his hand. I figured I needed to be as polite as I could to make up for my scraggly looking clothes. "Robert Jensen. I'm the new embalmer."

"Joe Kinney," said the cop. "Careful where you step, this area's still under investigation."

"Gotcha," I said, and stepped back. "Margo said it was another drowning?"

"That's what we think, at least," said Joe. He was writing something on his pad. "Guess the autopsy will tell us for sure."

"Kathy Schrenk didn't get an autopsy."

"Kathy Schrenk was an anomaly," said Joe. "Crabtree makes it a pattern."

"And how could you tell he drowned?"

Joe shrugged. "He was full of water. Seemed like a likely explanation. Came trickling out of him every time we tried to move him. Plus he was soaked to the bone, like we'd pulled him out of a river." He pointed at the dry dirt around the yellow card, tracing a wide oval in the air with his finger. "You can't see it now, but there was a whole patch of wet ground around him. This desert just drank it up, like it was running down a drain." He stared at the spot on the ground. "I don't know how the water got to him, but it did."

I stared with him and then looked at the yard again, wondering where an attacker might have come from. How were Rain's servants drowning people? How were they bringing in that much water and getting it into the victims? And for that matter, how were they choosing their victims? An old woman, an even older man, and me. It didn't make sense.

"Well would you look at that," said Joe. I glanced over at him and saw him crouch down, peering not at the ground by the marker, but at the rusted truck nearby. "I'll be damned."

"What?"

"Tracks in the dust," he said, pointing at the side of the truck. "This heap's been here probably thirty years—that's a '78 Ford—and probably only ever gets washed when it rains. But there's rivulets of water tracing all through the dust here, and this middle patch doesn't have any dust at all. It's been sprayed with water."

He was right, and once pointed out, it was impossible not to see it. The splash zone, or whatever it was that had gotten the truck wet, extended to the left onto a second truck—it hadn't been sprayed as heavily as the one by the body, but it had definitely gotten wet. Drops had hit the dirt and run down the metal, leaving long, clear trails in the layer of dust. We stood up, looking at the other cars stacked on top of these two; the splash pattern extended maybe ten feet up, exploding out like a ghost of fireworks frozen in dried mud.

"Robert!" called Margo from the doorway. "You coming in or not?"

I stared at the water pattern for a moment longer, then turned and walked to the house while Joe took pictures of this new clue.

How had water sprayed out like that? Which of Rain's minions had done it, and what method or tool had caused the splash? How, and why, did you drown someone like that?

I thought for one second that it might have been Shelley Jones herself, mind controlled into killing her own husband, but as soon as I reached the front door and saw her I discarded that idea. She was tiny and frail and used a walker to move painfully from the kitchen to the couch.

She sat down gently and then, with shaking hands, pulled a pair of small water bottles from the basket on the front of her walker.

"Have a drink," she said. "It's hot out."

I took the bottles and handed one to Margo.

"I don't know what I'm going to do now," said Shelley.

"You'll find something," said Margo, and twisted the top off her water bottle. She sat down on a sofa, and I sat next to her. "We all do."

"How do you manage?" asked Shelley. "Your husband passed away so long ago, and you've been so all alone."

"I have Harold," said Margo, and took a sip of water. "And Jasmyn. And Robert here. Robert, this is Shelley Jones."

I waved. "Hi."

"Good morning," said Shelley. She smiled, but it only lasted a second, and then the happiness drained back out of her face. "He was all I had, you know."

"Not that he was ever much worth having," said Margo.

My eyes opened wide in shock. Did she really just say that to a widow?

"He helped me remember the pills," said Shelley. "With this arthritis I can't even open the bottles on my own— what am I going to do now?"

"You can sell the yard," said Margo. "And the house. I don't imagine it's worth much as a business these days— you were mostly living on social security, anyway—but the state might want it. Not everyone's piped up for water and electricity this far out in the desert, and that's got to be worth something to somebody."

"And live in a home?" asked Shelley. "This is where I belong."

"You'll have more company in a rest home than you do out here," said Margo. "The only time you ever leave this place is to come to a funeral."

"Company," said Shelley. Her eyes got watery and the corners of her mouth turned down. "Company comes and goes, and nurses are only there because you pay them. I don't want company, and I never did."

"What do you want?" asked Margo.

"Matthew wasn't kind, but he was mine," said Shelley. "And we never had children, so now there's nothing of mine that's left to be had."

Margo laid her yellow folder on the coffee table and started going through the decisions for the funeral arrangements: what day, how big, do you want a viewing, do you want a graveside, do you want a burial or a cremation? I listened, but I wasn't paying close attention—something Shelley said had sparked an idea. Who were the drowning victims? Kathy, and Crabtree, and me. I'd thought we didn't have anything in common, but we did: not age, not location, not profession, not any of the typical demographic markers a serial killer used to pick their victims. But this wasn't a serial killer, it was a Withered, and the Withered had their own dark needs that the rest of us couldn't fathom. The drowning victims weren't linked by anything physical, but we had one powerful emotional similarity.

We were all alone.

Kathy Schrenk had had no family, no husband, no children. A sister and a few passing social friends, and that was it. Crabtree Jones had had a wife, but they obviously weren't very close, and out here in the desert they wouldn't have seen much of anyone else. And me? I had no one left at all, and my only friend was a thousand miles away, locked up in protective custody. I didn't have anyone I could talk to, or stay with, or be with, outside of a tiny handful of barely acquaintances. Margo was an employer, not a friend, and Parker only knew the false face I put on around others, and that only a little. We were all alone, and we had all been attacked.

Did Rain target lonely people because there was no one around to defend them? The only reason I'd lived through my attack was the unexpected appearance of help. It was possible that this was just a matter of convenience, choosing victims away from witnesses, but there was a difference between people who were alone and people who were temporarily by themselves. Every killer chose victims when no one was around; that was one thing. Rain was choosing victims who were deeply, perhaps fundamentally, alone, and that was another thing entirely. But what did it mean?

Shelley's arthritis was so bad she couldn't hold a pen, so Margo filled out the rest of the paperwork for her, walking

her through each decision on the funeral. The business of
death was, for many morticians, pure business: they pushed
the expensive options, they racked up the add-ons and extra fees, and they used your loved one's death to maximize
their personal profits. And I guess I couldn't blame them,
because that was their job—everyone's trying to make
money and someone has to bury the dead, so they might
as well make some money too, right? That had always been
my father's philosophy. But my mother had never been
like that, and Margo wasn't either; she walked Shelley
through the maze of choices calmly and honestly, explaining everything clearly and talking Shelley out of the more
superfluous luxuries. We left about an hour later, with a
modest funeral laid out on Margo's small stack of papers,
capped off with Shelley's credit card number written down
in Margo's neat block handwriting.

I took one last look at the crime scene, wondering again
where the water had come from and how it had splashed
so high, and then we got in the car and drove back to the
mortuary.

Jasmyn and Harold were already there, cleaning up but
mostly killing time; Luke Minaker's funeral wasn't for another day, and there was only so much prep work to be
done for it. Margo explained our visit to Crabtree and
then called the coroner, trying to get an idea of when we
might receive the body after the autopsy. I leaned against
the office wall, leaving the chair for Jasmyn, when suddenly my backpack, forgotten in the corner, started sing-

ing "Happy Birthday." It took me a second to realize what that meant, but then I grabbed my backpack and bolted from the room.

"Robert?" asked Jasmyn. "Are you okay?"

"Cell phone," I called back.

"Happy Birthday" meant the back door, so I ran to the front and looked out carefully. When I saw no cars or armed FBI task force, I slipped outside. The motion sensor in the garden saw me, and my backpack ding-donged, and I stuck close to the wall as I ran along the side of the building, headed toward the corner. It felt stupid, but I had to treat every alarm as the real deal or what good did they do me? If the FBI showed up to investigate the mysterious fire I'd be captured, and probably spend the rest of my life in jail; now that we had a pattern of impossible drownings, like the cop had said, the odds of FBI involvement were growing even higher. I couldn't let them see me. Honestly I needed to just leave the mortuary completely, but I was learning too much here. It was the best way I had to follow the trail of bodies, because the trail inevitably passed right through this building.

But how long until it got too dangerous to stay?

I peeked around the back of the building and saw one lone car in the parking lot; I couldn't tell the make, but it was old and foreign, and almost definitely not an FBI fleet vehicle. Could I risk going back in? I walked slowly to the back door, listening carefully, and heard Margo and Harold talking with someone. I glimpsed him through the gaps in a tree—older, probably Margo's age, but thin as a rail and wearing a suit. He had glasses and a briefcase. She seemed to be talking to him in a friendly enough manner, like she knew him, but his responses were odd—not rude, but standoffish. Above all else, he didn't *look* FBI; they had a way about them that was all too easy to spot once you'd spent a lot time with them. I watched a while longer, until my backpack chirped *ding-dong* again. Someone going in the front door, or coming out of it looking for me. I returned to the front of the building and reached the corner just as Jasmyn came around it.

"You okay?" she asked.

"Yeah," I said, patting my backpack. "It's nothing. Just my cell phone."

"Yesterday your ringtone was Christmas," she said. "Is it . . . your birthday today?"

"No, it's my friend's. From another town. Customized ringtone." I looked behind me, then back at Jasmyn. "Do you know who that is at the door?"

"Some friend of Margo's," said Jasmyn. "Mr. Connor; he didn't give a first name. I've never met him."

"Okay," I said, and nodded. I stood there for a moment, then nodded again. "Well, my phone call's done, so should we go back inside?"

Jasmyn shrugged, and we walked around to the back door. My backpack sang "Happy Birthday" again as we approached it, but I ignored it. "It's nothing," I told Jasmyn. "They can leave a message."

We found Margo and the newcomer in the office, talking about money. Margo looked up as we came in. "Jasmyn, Robert, this is Mr. Connor, an old friend of mine from before I moved to Lewisville. He's here to work on our books and get us on whatever this software's called."

"Quicken," said Mr. Connor. The wrinkles in his face were almost all vertical, which made him look solemn, like a slim cathedral. He walked past Margo to the chair behind the desk and sat without asking permission. "I can get started right now if you like."

"Thank you," said Margo. "Jasmyn, honey, can you run and get Mr. Connor a drink? What do you want, Mr. Connor, cola or lemon-lime?"

"Water will be fine," said Mr. Connor. He was already clicking away with the mouse.

"Run along, honey," said Margo. "Robert, walk with me a second."

Oh no.

Margo led me down the hall a bit, finding a secluded spot by a draped alcove, and looked at me seriously. "You seem awfully jumpy."

"Sorry."

"I don't want an apology, I want an explanation."

"My cell phone rang, and I had to go answer it."

"That doesn't sound like any cell phone I've ever heard, though I can't imagine what else it is. And it has an interesting habit of ringing every time somebody comes to our door."

"I hadn't noticed."

Margo stared at me a moment, like she was trying to read a book that was written on my face. "Do you know why I hired you?" she said at last.

"Because I'm very good at a job you need done."

"Because you need help," she said. "I saw it with Jasmyn and all the others, and I see it with you. Homeless and drifting and addicted. Sprinting out the door every time that phone rings. I don't know what you're running from, Robert, but I know you're running."

"I . . ." I didn't know what to say. That I was running from humans and monsters both? That I needed this job to help me find them first? Would any of that matter, even if she believed it? Maybe it was just time to move on. "I can get out of your way."

"I'm not asking you to get out of my way," she said. "I tell you you're running from something else and your first instinct is to run from me, and I understand that. You're not the first teenage drifter I've taken in and you won't be the last, though you're certainly the only one who could work a minor miracle on that third-degree burn victim's makeup yesterday. I don't want you to leave. What I'm asking you for, Robert, is a little trust. I don't need to know all your secrets any more than you need to know all of mine, but I can't help you if you don't tell me at least something."

I watched her, trying to decide what to say. "I don't really respond well to people trying to help me."

"Like I haven't noticed that."

How much could I tell her? If she really made a habit of helping troubled youth, surely she'd be accepting of a little strangeness? Obviously I couldn't tell her the whole truth, but maybe there was some portion of it that would calm her down and get her off my back?

"I left my family," I said. I guess my sister counted. "I don't want them to find me, so I'm . . . laying low."

She stared at me a while before responding. "That's not everything," she said at last.

"But it's true," I said. "The details can come out later."

She pursed her lips, considering me. "All right," she said at last. "Promise me you're not running drugs, or anything like that."

"I promise."

"And you're eighteen? Not a minor anymore?"

"Yes."

"Then I'll cover for you," she said. "But sooner or later you will need to tell me the rest of this story, so that I know what I'm covering and the best way to get you out from under it."

"Thank you," I said.

"I don't know how long it's been since somebody had your back," she said, "but I hope it helps you relax enough to get yourself together."

"Thank you," I said again. "I guess we'll see."

She nodded and walked away, and I thought about all the people who'd had my back before.

There was only a tiny handful of them still living or sane.

CHAPTER 10

If you want to drown somebody, you have to drown them in something, right? Simon Watts, under the sway of the Dark Lady, had tried to submerge me in the canal, and he or someone else had probably submerged Kathy Schrenk in something as well, even if it was only her head in a bucket. And if someone had brought a bucket to Crabtree—or probably something bigger, like a tub or a barrel—and then forced him into it, then that might explain the splash pattern we'd seen etched into the dust. His whole body had been soaked, so he'd obviously been immersed in something. Maybe he'd fought back and sprayed water everywhere. So that much was obvious: someone was using large quantities of water to kill people.

The bigger question was: why?

I looked at Jasmyn, who was pulling on a pair of latex gloves as we prepared to work on Crabtree's corpse. My backpack had dinged and beeped and sang occasionally over the last few days, but Margo was understanding of it, and she'd assured the others that they could be as well, so life had gone on, and now the body was here. I finished tying my apron and pulled on some gloves of my own.

"Why is she doing it?" I asked.

"Why is who doing what?" asked Jasmyn.

"The serial drowner," I said. "Why is she drowning them?"

"Why do you think it's a she?"

I couldn't exactly tell her about my inside information on Rain the Dark Lady, so instead I shook my head. "I've had about enough of your gender-normative stereotyping, young lady."

She raised her eyebrow. "Blaming this on a woman without any shred of evidence is not the proud blow for equality you seem to think it is."

"Excuse me for trying to be an ally."

"An ally to what?" asked Margo. She came into the room wearing full medical scrubs and a mask over her face, ready to get to work.

Jasmyn smirked. "Robert thinks our serial killer is a woman."

"And I suppose she might be," said Margo. "A serial killer can be a woman just as easily as a man."

"Are you saying that serial killers can change genders?" I asked. "Or that men in general can change genders? Your grammar was fuzzy."

"I'll knock you fuzzy," she said, and pointed at the body bag. "Open that with your teeth if it'll keep you from talking."

Jasmyn grabbed the zipper and pulled it open. "Do you think we'll see any black goo?"

Margo frowned at her. "Why do you ask that?"

"Robert said drowning victims have black goo."

Margo looked at me, and I shrugged. "I'm really bad at small talk."

Jasmyn looked at the corpse inside the bag. "Would you rather an alligator ate you, or a gorilla?" She pulled the zipper all the way to the bottom. "I'd rather the alligator ate the gorilla."

"What on earth has gotten into the two of you this morning?" asked Margo

"Grammar," I said.

Margo scowled and dismissed the topic with a contemptuous wave. "I'd rather the alligator ate both of you," she said, "but you're all I have, so get to work. Robert, help me slide that body bag out from under there. Jasmyn, get a towel over his privates." We moved the body around, getting it ready to work on it, and then pulled out the bag of organs. "Jasmyn, honey, you want this again?"

"I'd rather work on the arterial," she said. "I need the practice."

"Robert, then," said Margo. "Just help us clean it first."

After making sure the body is dead—which, again, the giant gaping *Y* incision rendered somewhat unnecessary— the next step in an embalming was to wash the corpse. This was even more important after an autopsy, because the body was likely to be covered in a variety of exciting chemicals. Margo scrubbed the bottom half and Jasmyn did the top while I got to work on the hair, which was my favorite part. I sprayed him liberally with the same disinfectant we'd used on the refrigerator and used a washrag to massage it into his scalp. I thought about the killings while I worked, and it always helped me to think out loud.

"So why?" I asked. "Male or female, whatever pronoun you want to use, why did the killer drown them?"

"Answering that question is not our job," said Margo.

"We're multitasking."

"I think he does it because he's sick," said Jasmyn. "I've . . . wanted to kill people before, but never old people. Never anyone harmless."

"Nobody's harmless," said Margo. "Obviously not Crabtree, but even Kathy had her faults."

Or they knew something, I thought. The wrong information in the wrong hands could be more harmful than any weapon, and I knew that I, at least, was certainly guilty of snooping around in Rain's affairs. That might be why she'd come after me. Maybe Kathy and Crabtree had done the same?

But again: why the drowning?

"Okay," I said. "Let's get technical about this. The central question of criminal profiling is: what did the killer do that they didn't have to do?"

Margo looked at me, long and hard, but she didn't say anything.

"Criminal profiling?" asked Jasmyn. "Your hobbies are way cooler than mine."

"I grew up in a mortuary," I said. "We saw a lot of murders, and I got curious about the detectives who solved them."

Margo raised her eyebrow.

"The killer is drowning them," I said. "Why?"

"We don't even know how," said Jasmyn.

"How doesn't matter yet," I said. "Why tells us more."

"Maybe you should ask yourself where," said Margo, looking back down at the legs she was scrubbing. "There certainly wasn't anywhere to drown anybody in the middle of that junkyard."

"What about Kathy's place?" I asked.

"Kathy was a friend of mine," said Margo, "I'd prefer not to speculate on her death."

"The kitchen sink," said Jasmyn. "A pot of water. The bathtub."

"Was her whole body soaked?" I asked. "Like Crabtree was?"

Jasmyn nodded. "Yep."

"Then the bathtub's a possibility," I asked. "You'd need something big. But they didn't find her in the bathtub, they found her in the living room. And there was nothing around there that could have drowned her."

"So they moved her," said Jasmyn.

"Exactly," I said. "So: why? They didn't have to move her, but they did. Were they trying to take her somewhere and gave up? Were they trying to pose her? Some serial killers ritualize the bodies, but Kathy hadn't been messed with—the cops didn't even think it was foul play until Crabtree showed up dead the same way."

"I will ask you more directly this time to stop talking about my friend," said Margo.

I nodded. "Fair enough. So Crabtree, then. He wasn't moved, but he was still drowned. And he wasn't anywhere near a sink or a bathtub, so it can't have been easy." I gestured at the frail old body in front of us. "There must be a hundred different ways to kill a decrepit old man like this, so why pick the hardest one?"

"It doesn't make sense," said Jasmyn.

"It always makes sense," I said. "We just don't know how until we find all the pieces and put them together."

"Crabtree was a bastard," said Margo, "but Kathy wasn't. No one would kill her on purpose, so maybe this is all a bunch of accidents."

Maybe it was—not all of the Withered enjoyed what they did, and some of them went out of their way to live peacefully, but accidents did happen. Simon Watts's attack on me wasn't anything like an accident. Not that I could tell them that.

"I thought you didn't want to talk about Kathy," said Jasmyn.

"Nothing salacious," said Margo. "All I'm saying is that she was a good woman."

"So what if it was an accident?" asked Jasmyn. "Someone accidentally drowned Kathy, and then he—or she—or whoever, it might not even be the same person—decided to kill Crabtree and went out of their way to use the same weird method, to make people think it was the same killer as the first one. So it's more likely that it wasn't the same person, just someone trying to throw the police off the trail with a fake serial killer." She looked at me. "Okay, I can see how you got into this; it's fun."

"There's nothing fun about death," said Margo.

"Says the woman holding a corpse's ankle," I said.

"This is serious," said Margo. "Why do you think I do this?"

"You've made jokes in the embalming room before," said Jasmyn.

"A little levity to lighten the mood is one thing," said Margo. "But you can fling mud or you can wallow in it, and all wallowing does is get you filthy."

"You do this because somebody has to," I said. "The mortuary, the funerals, the visits to the widows. You do it because death is everywhere and nobody wants to deal with it, but if you do it then at least it gets done right. The bodies get respect, and the family gets some peace of mind, and Shelley Jones gets the right kind of flowers on the casket. You do it because you're the only one who can."

"And why do you do it?" she asked, and I knew from her eyes that she wasn't just asking about the mortuary. She was asking about my ideas, and my investigation, and my weird singing backpack, and my drifting, and my running, and my everything. She was asking like she knew what it meant to ask it.

"Same reason," I said.

We watched each other for a moment, and then Jasmyn broke the silence. "I do it because I like washing dead people," she said. "Don't bother yourselves finishing your parts of the job—that's all the more dead person for me to spend my entire afternoon scrubbing down with a baby brush."

"Sorry," I said. "I'll get back to work."

I took a soft comb and ran it through Crabtree's hair, over and over, slow and easy, though he didn't have much left. I combed out the gunk at the base of the hair—we all have it, whether we notice it or not—and then rinsed his whole head with a spray nozzle hooked up to the sink. The soap ran down and into the drains built into the table, and Crabtree was cleaner than he might have ever been.

Maybe Jasmyn was right about the killer pulling a fake out. Not trying to convince us she was a serial

killer, because why would Rain care about that? But trying to convince somebody, somewhere, that the deaths
were supernatural. Simon Watts had been ordered to
drown me, but then what? Was he going to move me?
Had Kathy been drowned in the canal as well, and then
moved to her living room where it was sure to look bi-
zarre? The police had called it an accident and gone on
their way, but I'd come straight here. What had the
killer done that she didn't have to do? She'd made a
run-of-the-mill killing, to use Jasmyn's term, look like a
Withered attack. And the only reason to do that was to
attract the attention of someone who knew about the
Withered.

Rack had done the same basic thing: hidden the nature of his own kills in order to trick and trap us. We were
hunting him, so he'd gathered an army and hunted us
back. A shadow war. Now Rain, maybe, was doing the
same thing.

I'd already seen Assu, and I knew for a fact the Withered were gathering. Maybe she was starting the war again,
and these drownings were the first shot fired.

"We Wish You A Merry Christmas" blared loudly from
my backpack, and I grabbed it and ran.

"Robert!" shouted Jasmyn.

"Quiet," said Margo. "You let me do the talking."

"To who?" and Jasmyn.

I stopped in the hall, holding my breath and listening.
The receiving door opened, and a man's voice called out.

"Knock knock," he said. "Can I come in?"

"Depends on who you are," said Margo.

"My name's Agent Harris, and I'm with the FBI. Do you mind if I ask you some questions?"

CHAPTER 11

I didn't move a muscle.

"The FBI," said Margo. "And what does the FBI want with the Ottessen Brothers Funeral Home?"

"Just some questions," said the agent. As with Simon Watts, I could tell that I knew this voice from somewhere, but I couldn't quite place it. None of the FBI agents I'd known or worked with had been named Harris. "I understand you had a pretty nasty fire in here recently."

"You can see the damage on the wall behind you," said Margo. "Are you here to investigate the arson?"

"Among other things," said the agent. "Do you happen to know who first found the fire?"

"My brother-in-law did," said Margo. "Harold Ottessen, though I suppose technically the fire alarm went off even before he got here, and that alerted the fire department. We've already given all the information to the fire marshal and the police."

"You did!" said the agent. His voice was cheerful, almost, which was a strange contrast to the dour stereotype most FBI agents tended to fall into. And frustratingly familiar. "You definitely did," he continued, "and I have no reason to doubt that report. I'm just crossing various *i*'s and dotting some *t*'s. I couldn't help but notice you've got a small apartment on the side of the building—that's common with mortuaries, isn't it? A holdover from the days of the old family business. Is there anyone living there at the moment?"

"Mr. Connor's in there now," said Jasmyn. "But back during the fire it was—"

"Empty," said Margo. "Mr. Connor's only staying here a few days. Before the fire Jasmyn lived in the room—this is Jasmyn Shahi, by the way, she's my assistant here—but she moved out on her own a few months ago."

I couldn't see them, but I imagined Margo had given Jasmyn a subtle signal of some kind, reinforcing her order of silence. Jasmyn didn't offer any more information.

"I see," said Harris. "And during the time of the fire, is there anybody who might have had access to the room or the building? Someone who might have been able to get inside here before the firefighters showed up?"

"You mean aside from the arsonist?" asked Margo. "Or the arsonist herself?"

"Herself? You think it's a woman?"

"I'm using a generic pronoun," said Margo. "Women can be arsonists if they want to be."

She said it right this time.

"Let me show you why I'm asking," said Harris. "Maybe this will clear things up, maybe jog your memory a little. This is a photo the local police took of the burned refrigerator, after the fire was put out. Do you see this here on the . . . well I'm afraid I don't know the lingo. What do you call that?"

"That's the slab," said Margo. "It's like a metal tray that slides in and out; it's what the body goes on."

"Thank you," said Harris. "The slab. Do you see this here on the slab? This kind of . . . pattern, I guess you'd call it. What would you say that looks like?"

"Ash," said Margo. "Makes sense, given there was a fire in there."

"Ash, yes," said Harris. "Definitely, but what shape is it? You, um, Jasmyn, was it? What would say that looks like?"

Jasmyn paused a minute before speaking. "A smear."

"A smear," said Harris. "That's exactly what I thought it looked like as well: a curved smear. And that seemed very strange to me, because a smear is not a pattern that one would expect to find at the scene of a fire, because it's not a shape that fires or fire hoses—which are the two dominant forces acting on the scene of a fire—would typically create. It looks almost like somebody wiped the slab, like they were trying to clean it off. So this being an arson, rather than a free-range organic fire, we may well be looking at a third force: human intervention."

"You think somebody lit a fire in my corpse fridge and then cleaned up after herself," said Margo. "May all our criminals be so civic-minded."

"Two witnesses reported a car speeding away from the scene," said Harris, "just as the firefighters were pulling up. Now it makes a certain kind of sense that an arsonist would choose to light a fire in what you lead me to believe is called a corpse fridge: garbage cans and Dumpsters and other metal containers are far and away the most popular places for urban fires because they contain the flames, and this is just a strange but very specific version of that. But I noticed on my way in here that you have a Dumpster in the back, which makes the choice of a corpse fridge much harder to account for. What kind of person would break all the way into a mortuary to light his or her fire in this specific location, and then delay leaving long enough to clean up after him or herself on the way out?"

"I can't say that I know," said Margo, and as bad as I was at reading vocal emotions, even I could tell that her voice was as cold as ice.

"I don't know either," said Harris, "though my working theory is that it was someone who had a connection to the mortuary—mortuaries in general, and this one specifically, given that the fire alarm was the only one that went off. You did say you have a security system, right?"

Margo paused for several moments before answering. "Yes."

"And yet the intruder alarms, the perimeter alarms, none of those went off. Implying that whoever lit that fire had access to the building."

Crap.

The room was silent for a while, and I wondered what was happening—they were all just staring at each other awkwardly, I guess—but I didn't dare to peek in. After a moment Harris spoke again.

"Just two more questions, ma'am, and then I can be out of your hair. The first is a favor: do you mind if I look in that drain by your feet?"

"I mind very much," said Margo.

"What do you think you'll find in the drain?" asked Jasmyn.

"Horrors beyond imagining," said Harris, "given that it's the floor drain in an embalming room. As it happens, though, I do have a search warrant, so asking your permission was mostly a formality." I heard rustling papers, and Margo muttered something, and then they all went silent for a moment. I imagined that Harris was kneeling down and unscrewing the grate on the drain, and took the risk of peeking in while he was distracted. He was indeed kneeling, facing away from me, his head hunched down over the drain in the floor. From this angle I couldn't see enough of him to make a clear identification, though I could at least confirm that he was young. Margo and Jasmyn were focused intently on his work, and none of the three saw me. I ducked back out of sight and a moment later heard the metallic clink as Harris lifted the grate and set it on the tiles. I heard the snap of a rubber glove and Jasmyn's groan of disgust. "That's the stuff," said Agent Harris. "Perfect. Jasmyn, would you be so kind as to open that plastic evidence bag next to me on the floor? I don't want to get this on the outside of it."

There was only one thing he could be looking for in the drain: soulstuff. Whoever this was knew about the Withered, and knew that one had died here. He was probably tipped off by the smear on the slab—I kicked myself mentally for doing such a crappy job of cleaning it up. I heard him take the glove off and then handle the bag; he'd probably just put the glove, soulstuff and all, inside the bag and sealed it up.

"There," he said. "Now, on to question number two. Which pocket did I put that in—ah, here it is. Do you know this young man? He may be going by the name John, or David, or I guess really anything. He changes it a lot."

Damn. Damn damn damn, around the parking lot and back in for another damn.

"He doesn't look familiar," said Margo. "Is he an arsonist?"

"And a mortician," said Harris. "So this is really right in his wheelhouse. You're sure you haven't seen him?"

"Pretty sure."

"You haven't . . . given him a job and a room in the back?"

Another damn. Who could have told him? The police—I would have been a part of the statement Margo gave to the police. And since Harris had already been to the local court, since he had a search warrant, it made sense he'd talked to the local cops, too.

"We had a boy for a day or two," said Margo, "but he wasn't here the night of the fire. And he's gone now."

"And he didn't look like this?"

"These old eyes don't work too well anymore," said Margo.

"What about you?" asked Harris. "Is this the boy?"

"You white people all look alike to me," said Jasmyn, and I'd never wanted to high five someone so hard in all my life.

"I see," said Harris. "Well then. Thanks for the floor-drain muck, and I'll be on my way. If you happen to remember anything else, here's my card, please give me a call."

"You can count on it," said Margo. "Thanks for coming."

I realized in sudden horror that the chime in my backpack would make a loud noise the instant he stepped outside, and I was standing close enough that he might hear it. I started creeping away as quietly as I could, wondering how fast I could go without creaking a floorboard or sounding an audible footstep and terrified that I wasn't going fast enough. I tried to get as far away as I could, an impossible combination of fast and silent, all the while scrambling to open my backpack and turn the chime off. I unzipped it and looked in, and realized that I had no idea which chime was which, or what sound they might make when I shut them down. The backpack chimed suddenly—"We Wish You A Merry Christmas"—and I prayed that the agent hadn't heard it. If he was already outside I didn't have to sneak anymore, so I sprinted at full speed and got to the window just in time to see the man walk out to his car: a black SUV with a Nebraska license plate. The agent turned back one more time, and I caught a clear glimpse of his face as I ducked out of sight.

Agent Mills. Or at least that's how he'd introduced himself, but I'd known at the time that was probably a fake name. Harris might be fake as well. He was the agent who'd caught up to Brooke and me in Dillon—an FBI analyst who specialized in serial killers and, more recently, the Withered. And me, by extension. No one else had ever been able to find me, but now Mills had done it twice. If he was here, the only move I had left might be to run.

But I was so close! I couldn't just leave. Especially not if the FBI was moving in on Lewisville—the last two times they'd come hunting Withered, they'd gone way overboard, filling the city with cops and SWAT and soldiers and guns, and it had ended poorly both times. If Rain and her army of monsters were really starting a shadow war, a huge government response could bring it out into the daylight.

The SUV drove away, and almost instantly I heard Margo calling my name: "Robert!" I ignored her and ran through the halls to the front door; I had to see which way Mills turned when he left the mortuary. He'd obviously already spoken to the local police—he had their crime-scene photos and a local search warrant. That meant that he had three obvious leads to follow up on next if he wanted to find me: Kathy Schrenk, Luke Minaker, and Crabtree Jones. The three Withered victims. If he turned right, he was headed to the highway, out to Crabtree; if he turned left he was headed to one of the other two. The only other people who'd seen me were the men at the bar and Jasmyn's friends, and Mills had no way to link them to me. I got to the front door with seconds to spare and watched as Mills turned left, into the center of town.

"Robert!" said Margo, shuffling up behind me. "You want to tell me what's going on?"

"Thank you for covering for me. I'm leaving now."

"That man had a picture of you," she said. Jasmyn stood next to her. "Did you light that fire?"

"I did not." I watched Mills's car drive away, disappearing out of sight behind a row of houses. I looked at Margo. "Yes, he was looking for me, but no I didn't do anything he said I did."

"What did you do?"

"You're better off not knowing."

"Which one is your real name?" asked Jasmyn.

I looked at her, terrified of telling the truth. . . .

. . . But I couldn't bring myself to lie to her. "John." That one word had the power to unravel everything I'd worked for, if she wanted to.

Her voice was quiet. "Did you hurt somebody, John?"

I stared back for far too long before I answered. "No one who didn't deserve it."

Margo started to talk, but I cut her off. "You won't see me again. And you should probably get out of town."

"I have a funeral to take care of," said Margo.

"The man you just met is . . . well, not a bad man, but like a bad omen." I tried to find the right words to make her believe me—which meant it couldn't be the whole truth, but it had to be a version of it. "Let me put it this way: there's a group in Lewisville. Think of it like a cartel, though this is not about drugs. Agent Harris is hunting that group, and that group does not like to be hunted. There will be *trouble*, and please understand that while that word is one hundred percent accurate in meaning, it's maybe only two percent accurate in scale. Many, many people will get hurt, and I don't want you to be one of them. You're good people."

"You're going to do something stupid," said Margo. "I can see it in your eyes, and I know what trouble-eyes look like."

"Maybe," I said. "Eventually. First things first: I'm doing exactly what I told you to do. I'm disappearing."

I pushed open the door, and my backpack chimed as I walked away.

CHAPTER 12

Mills would be going one of two places: the Schrenk family or the Minaker family. Which one? I didn't know much about Mills, but I knew he was smart—smart enough to deduce that one of the Withered was already dead. He'd found the soulstuff and connected it to the fire, so he could guess that the dead Withered was the fire one. Plus we'd had another drowning, so he'd know that the drowner was still active. He'd want to talk to the first drowning victim's family, so Schrenk it was.

I should run, I told myself. *I should head straight to the highway and get out of town, waiting until the heat cools off*

*before sticking my nose back into the middle of Lewisville.
That would be the smart thing to do.*

*But then people might die, and I can't let that happen. Not
if I'm here to do something about it.*

I turned left and followed Mills into town.

Kathy Schrenk's house was empty and maybe even sold,
but her sister Carol was still around and the closest family
Kathy had. Carol only lived about a mile away from the
mortuary, by a hill, and the Lewisville canal made the road
to get there much longer than that. If I cut through some
yards and jumped a few fences, I could be there before
Mills could. I started running, strapping my backpack
tightly and buckling the waist belt to keep it from flop-
ping up and down as I ran. I tried to keep the overhead
view in my mind as I ran, remembering which streets and
cross streets went where, and circumventing almost all of
them by vaulting my way through yards and gardens. I
reached the canal and stashed my backpack by a culvert—
I could come back for it later—and then dove in, swim-
ming across and trying not to think about what might be
in the water. On the far side I got lost in a maze of identi-
cal suburban houses, but only for a few minutes. I found
Carol Schrenk's house just as Agent Mills knocked on the
door, and I watched from the edge of a fence at the corner of the road as Carol let him in.

I waited until I was sure he wouldn't see me, then
slipped across the street and crept up to the house. I found

an open window, half filled with a whirring swamp cooler, and stood beneath it and listened.

". . . what I'll do," said Carol. "Kathy was all I had."

"I'm very sorry for your loss," said Agent Mills. "I've heard great things about her."

"What is today?" she asked. "Monday? Kathy used to come over every Monday night. We'd knit together. I was working on an afghan, but now I guess there's no point finishing it."

"Was it for Kathy?"

"It wasn't really for anybody. I suppose there's got to be somebody around the neighborhood who might want it, but I suppose none of them would miss it, either, if I never got it done."

"Ms. Schrenk, can I show you a picture? I'm wondering if you might have seen this boy anywhere. The police say he has a job working at the funeral home."

Crap. So he knew Margo and Jasmyn were lying.

"Oh, I don't know," said Carol. "I don't want to get involved in any trouble."

"He's not in trouble, ma'am, he's missing."

I shook my head, marveling at Mills's ability to pick up so quickly on what made Carol tick. She didn't want to say anything—it was even possible that Margo had already called, warning her to stay quiet—but once Mills presented me as a missing person instead of a fugitive, it pushed all of her I'm-so-lonely buttons. He dropped a kicker at the end, just to make sure. "His sister is searching everywhere for him. Their mother passed away a few years ago, and he's all she has left."

"That's terrible," said Carol. "Are they from Lewisville?"

"They're not," said Mills, "but we have strong evidence that he might be here now. At the funeral home, like I said. Did you happen to see him at your sister's funeral?"

"I think so," said Carol. "In fact, now that I think about it, I'm certain he was at my Kathy's funeral. He stood in the back with Jasmyn, and then again at the graveside service."

"With Jasmyn?" he asked. So now he was even more certain that Jasmyn had lied. "Is he dating her?"

Why did everyone think I was dating her?

"He'd be foolish not to," said Carol. "She's such a sweet girl, and so lovely."

"Do you know Jasmyn Shahi well?"

"Only through Kathy. Kathy worked at the mortuary, you know, and sometimes I'd visit her and talk to the other employees. Jasmyn is quiet, but she's a darling."

"Do you happen to know where she lives?" asked Agent Mills. "I'd love to talk to her."

"I'm afraid I only talked to her a few times, and only in passing. I don't talk to people easily, and she's so young. What am I going to say to a young girl like that?"

"Who do you talk to?"

"Now that Kathy's passed away? No one."

It occurred to me, listening to Carol Schrenk talk, that

she was even lonelier than her sister. At least Kathy had had a job, and friends, and things to do; Carol had nothing. I'd theorized that Rain was killing lonely people, but if that was true then she'd gotten the wrong sister. And Shelley Jones, as well—at least Crabtree, hated as he was, saw people. He'd come into town to go shopping and whatever else he did. Shelley had never gone anywhere. Was Rain killing the *families* of lonely people, instead of the lonely people themselves? Was she trying to make them lonelier? Who was she trying to hurt by killing me?

"Do you have any of Kathy's belongings?" asked Mills. "Perhaps a calendar or day planner or something? A cell phone?"

"I have a few things," said Carol. "Will a box of photos help?"

"Ideally I need something with notes in it," said Mills, "maybe an address book? A . . . Rolodex? I don't know, anything that might have names or phones numbers."

"She kept a planner," said Carol, "but it was in her house, and the bank is taking care of that. The estate and everything."

"Do you have access to it?"

"I've never asked," said Carol. "It would only make me sad to go through her things like that."

Mills grumbled, a low sigh that was half growl. "Can you give me the name of the bank? And I guess we may as well look at those photos, then, if that's all you've got."

"I've got them right here," said Carol, and I heard her

chair creak as she rose to her feet and shuffled slowly across the floor. The photos would be useless—he was just being nice at this point—but sooner or later he'd find something, and through it he'd find me. The bank would give him Kathy's things, or he'd push harder on Jasmyn and get her to give up some info. I didn't want to leave town, but maybe I had to. With the full weight of the FBI behind him, how could Mills *not* find me?

"Who's this?" asked Mills. "This girl standing next to Jasmyn?"

"One of her little friends from college," said Carol. "I forget her name, because it's so hard to spell. Something with an exclamation point."

This just kept getting worse.

"An exclamation point in her name?"

"Replacing one of the 'i's," said Carol. "L!sa? El!sa? Al!cia, that's what it is. Kids these days."

"Tell me about it," said Mills.

If he could find Al!sha, then he could find Parker, and eventually he'd find where I was staying. They wouldn't cover for me like Jasmyn had—they'd spill everything, and eagerly, especially if they thought they were protecting their friend from some dangerous drifter she'd gotten messed up with. I had to leave.

I didn't wait for Mills to finish his conversation with Carol. I jumped the back fence into the neighbor's yard, went to the culvert to retrieve my backpack, and then walked toward the edge of town. The highway to the

Crabtree Junkyard went west, so I went east. I could come back later, when the hunt had died down.

In the Midwest, a town like this would trickle out slowly, surrounded by farmland or ranchland or some other business trying to make use of the prairie. Arizona has no prairie to make use of, so when the city ended it ended abruptly: the houses stopped, and the desert started, and the road wound slowly toward the red-rock canyons. I walked out a good half hour, curving around a couple of low hills, and then stood in the shade of a saguaro cactus trying to thumb a ride. Nobody stopped. I pulled a ball cap from my backpack and pulled it low over my eyes, trying to protect my head from the sun, and wished that I'd brought some water with me.

The truck I'd rode in on when I'd first come to Lewisville had passed a couple of restaurants and a gas station a few miles outside of town, at the mouth of one of the canyon trailheads, so I started walking again, thinking I could hitch a ride more easily out there. I made the trip in about an hour, and drank water ravenously from the faucet in the bathroom sink. A few people stopped for gas, but they were all just on day trips out from Lewisville, here to go hiking and then head home again. Useless to me as transportation. I hung around for as long as I dared, and when the clerks got too suspicious, I headed out again, going east across the desert. If I didn't manage to catch a ride by nightfall . . . well, it wouldn't be the first time I'd slept outside. The road rejoined the canal, or some other canal that fed into or out of it, and I walked for a time in the shade of the trees that grew along the banks.

Twilight was just starting to fall when I saw a girl in the shadows ahead.

She was moving oddly, almost furtively, like she was a wild animal sniffing for predators on the wind. Or prey. She wore a skirt and some kind of a blouse, and as I drew closer I saw that it was ragged. Almost instantly I recognized her: the homeless girl from the viewing. Run from Rain. It wasn't a skirt and blouse but an old A-line dress, so out of fashion even I could tell it was strange. Her hair was wild and tangled, and her feet were bare.

She looked up suddenly and stared at me from thirty yards away. I stopped walking and held myself motionless. She cocked her head and swayed softly, never taking her eyes off of me.

"Hello," I called out. "Do you remember me?" She'd asked me before if I knew her, or if she knew me. I couldn't remember exactly. When she saw me now, would she remember me from the viewing? Or would she remember whoever she thought I was?

She didn't say anything.

I walked a little closer.

"I was at the viewing," I said. "Kathy Schrenk. Did you know her or did you just walk in?"

She sniffed again, three quick breaths through her nose. I stopped walking, and she circled me warily. She looked like she was thirty or so, weathered by the elements but not as much as I'd expected. How long had she been homeless? And why was she out here, so far from the city?

"Are you okay?" I asked. "What's your name?"

She opened her mouth and hissed.

The woman I'd met at the viewing had been bedraggled but lucid—she'd looked uncomfortable in the room, but not scared by it. Our conversation had been short and confusing, but it had been intelligible. She'd been smart and alert and human. This woman seemed completely feral.

"Are you okay?" I asked again. "When's the last time you ate?" Had she been out here alone in the desert this whole time? Did she have heat exhaustion, or maybe even heat stroke? What had happened to her mind?

She continued to circle me, moving out onto the highway as if the barrier between dirt and road meant nothing to her. I shrugged my backpack off of one shoulder and she froze, watching me cautiously, though I couldn't tell if she was getting ready to run or attack. I slowly opened the zipper on my backpack and rooted inside of it for a pack of fruit leather. I still had a little left from my last time on the road, the bag carefully folded around the few strips that remained. When I pulled it out she sniffed again, so like an animal I couldn't help but frown and take a step backward. Who was she? *What* was she? And what had happened to her?

Her eyes fixed on the bag of fruit leather and she stepped forward, keeping her knees bent and her posture low. I unfolded the well-worn bag and pulled out a piece and held it out to her as far as my arm would reach. "I don't have any water, but if you need food you can have it." She took a few more steps, until her outstretched arm could just reach mine, and snatched the fruit leather from my hand. She smelled it, but kept her eyes on me. She didn't eat it.

Is this what Rain did to the minds she controlled? Use them so much they got completely used up? Is this what Simon Jacob Watts could look forward to, after years or months or even just days of mind control? An atrophied brain that couldn't control itself without a powerful Withered intelligence guiding its every move?

I pulled another piece of leather from the bag. "It's food," I said. "You eat it. Go ahead." I gestured toward her, and her eyes darted back and forth between me and the leather. "Look, like this." I put the fruit leather in my mouth, trying to tear off a piece to show her, when suddenly she lunged, howling like a cat and snarling in a vicious grin that showed off every filthy jagged tooth. I stumbled back but she was already on me, clawing at my hands and mouth with her chipped fingernails, snapping her teeth and hissing, clutching at the leather and the bag of fruit leather with terrifying ferocity. I let go of both, just trying to stop her from biting me, shouting at her to stop while her nails dug deep, bloody grooves in my arms. Suddenly she lit up, like a bright light was shining on her, and she looked up with that same animal alertness. A truck was coming toward us on the highway. She let go of me and sprinted toward the canal, disappearing into the trees and undergrowth. I clambered back to my feet, keeping my eyes on the bushes, and frantically motioned for the truck to stop. I was standing in the middle of the road, so it did. The driver rolled down the passenger window.

"I need to get out of here," I said, still watching the bushes. "She just attacked me." I picked up my backpack from where it had fallen in the scuffle. "I don't care where you're going. Just let me ride in the back, I just need to get out of here."

"Oh come on, John, as long as we've known each other? You can ride up front with me."

I turned slowly, already recognizing the voice. He sat in the driver's seat looking far too pleased with himself.

"Agent Mills."

"Didn't you hear?" he said. "It's Agent Harris now."

"How'd you find me?"

"I'm a psychological profiler, John, give me some credit. You knew I was looking for you, and you knew what would happen when I found you. Obviously you'd run the first chance you got, and there's only one major highway in and out of town, and the west route goes toward a key crime scene. This is the road you'd be least likely to accidentally be seen on, so this is the road I looked on."

"I don't like being predictable."

"You're not going to like anything that happens over the next few days," said Mills. "May as well get used to it now."

"I could run."

"Do it: I have a stun gun which I am practically giddy to try out."

I sighed. I was exhausted and scared and hopped up on adrenaline, not to mention bleeding from who knew how many gashes in my forearms. "Do you have water?"

"And curly fries," said Mills. "I stopped at that gas station a ways back to ask if anyone had seen you."

I laughed drily. "Barbecue sauce?"

"Ranch."

"Philistine." I looked back at the bushes. Who was she? How did she fit into all this?

She'd tried to kill me, and, for all I knew, eat me. It was too much.

"All right," I said, and opened the door. "Whatever cell you throw me into, make sure it has a bed. I haven't slept in days."

"Only the finest for my favorite fugitive," said Mills. I got in and closed the door, and he turned the SUV around in a slow, three-point turn. "Back to Lewisville first, though. We have unfinished business."

CHAPTER 13

I lay back in the passenger seat, too exhausted to run anymore. The air conditioner was going full blast, and I reached out and turned it off.

"Are you crazy?" asked Mills. "It's like a million degrees out there."

"I know," I said, closing my eyes. "I just came in from it. Let me adjust a little before you freeze me to death."

"Have some water," he said, and nodded toward a pair of plastic water bottles in the cup holders. One was still sealed, so I twisted off the cap and drank eagerly. "Who was the girl?"

"You saw her?"

"Of course I saw her, did you think she was a mirage?"

I held up my lacerated arms, which were starting to sting so badly it felt like they were burning. "You know, I'd wondered where these wounds came from. This all makes so much sense now."

"Is she another victim?"

I opened one eye and looked at him. "You know that too?"

"Who else would you be fighting with in the middle of nowhere?"

I opened my other eye and sat up straight. "So wait. If you knew she was part of the case, why didn't you stop and try to find her?"

"Operational priorities," said Mills. "Find and retrieve John Cleaver, above all else."

"I can't be that important."

"I don't know. How many people have you killed?"

"People or Withered?"

"How about people you thought were Withered?"

"Everyone I've ever killed has dissolved into sludge," I said. "So I'm either innocent or I'm deeply psychotic."

"Already laying the grounds for an insanity plea," Mills said, and sniffed away a fake tear. "They grow up so fast."

"I'm serious," I said. "You know that I don't hurt actual people." I paused, then shook my head. "Obviously not counting Nathan, but that was self-defense."

"On purpose," said Mills.

"What? I told you before, it was self-defense."

"I'm not talking about Nathan," said Mills. "Screw that guy. Nobody at the bureau liked him anyway. I'm just saying you don't hurt people *on purpose*."

"So now you think I accidentally murdered somebody?"

"I think that Brooke Watson will spend the rest of her life in mental care."

"That's not my fault."

"Not directly," said Mills. "Those dead kids in Dillon weren't directly your fault, either. And neither was Fort Bruce. And neither was Marci or your mom."

"Let me out," I said, unbuckling my belt in the speeding SUV. "I'd rather take my chances with the stun gun."

"I know that was a low blow," said Mills, "and I'm sorry, but that's the reality."

"I said let me out."

"You're dangerous."

"I was trying to save people," I said. "I did save people."

"Only indirectly."

"That doesn't count?"

"Why should the indirect good things count when you don't want to count the indirect bad ones?"

I glowered but sank back in my chair. My actions, in killing the Withered, had stopped those Withered from killing anybody else, and that was good; it had saved lives. But that single-minded crusade had also endangered a lot of people and left some of them dead. The math worked out in my favor—a couple of dead bystanders versus a thousand future victims—but did that really matter? Did that really make it okay? At the end of the day, people were still dead because of me.

"I'm not trying to hurt you," said Mills.

"Well that makes it all okay then."

"Society cannot function the way you seem to want it to," said Mills. "We have rules and procedures and balances, and when monsters need to be killed—because monsters are totally real, and sometimes they totally need to be killed—we have people in place to kill them. We have police and detectives and militaries and intelligence agencies, and governments and laws to control their use."

"And before I came along," I said, "none of those things were remotely effective against the monsters."

"I realize that."

"Agent Ostler said that in the entire history of the FBI they'd never actually killed one. I killed one *last week*, and he wasn't even the one I was looking for."

"Being good at something you're not supposed to do does not make it a good thing to do."

"You sound like my mother."

"Well, somebody needs to."

"Are you seriously saying that it's better to let the Withered prey on the human race than to break a few rules in order to stop them?"

"I'm saying that you can work within the rules and get the same results."

"We tried that before," I said. "We got Fort Bruce. What was the final death count?"

"You're just as bad as they are," said Mills loudly. "There, you made me say it. Are you happy now? Does that clear this up for you? You're running around, loose and unsupervised, leaving death and madness and chaos in your path, and the United States government cannot allow that to happen. Stopping that from happening is, in fact, our entire job. And it doesn't matter if you have an excuse, or if you're being effective, or if you're the lesser of two evils. You're still one of the evils." He paused, watching the road ahead. "I didn't even come to Lewisville looking for you, I was investigating a statistically significant occurrence of mysterious deaths. I was looking for monsters, and I found you. And that should tell you something."

"They're raising an army," I said.

"That's what you told us before."

"They're going to start a war."

"You said that before, too."

"And I was right," I said. "And you know I was."

"That war has come and gone," said Mills. "You took out Rack, and you took out his stragglers, and whatever tiny scattering of Withered is left is not capable of mounting a war."

"You haven't met them yet."

"Who could possibly be left?" asked Mills. "Rack recruited all the useful ones, or at least most of them. He never got Mr. Burns, but now you've taken care of him, so who's left?"

" 'Mr. Burns?' "

"The fire guy," said Mills. "Bureau nickname."

"That's a little on-the-nose."

"They can't all be the Son of Sam," said Mills. "Sometimes you have cool names, and sometimes you have Mr. Burns."

"So, what's your plan?" I asked. "Bring in another army, like you did in Dillon?"

"And what's your response?" asked Mills. "Tell us that's too dangerous because of a mind controller?"

I rolled my eyes. "Yes, dammit, but that's . . . not . . ."

"Great," said Mills, "another mind-control monster."

"It's not the same one."

"It's not *any* one," said Mills. "The Withered in Dillon wasn't a mind controller, it was like a big crazy yeti thing."

"So, I was wrong," I said. "I still got her, and I'm still right about this one. That feral woman you didn't want to look for was one of her victims—her mind was so broken by control that's she's barely even sentient anymore."

"And naturally you have no proof of this."

"It's my current theory," I said. "So far it seems to be holding up."

"That's not a theory," said Mills, "that's a hunch. You'd know the difference if you'd ever, you know, gone through formal investigative training, or really any schooling whatsoever, past tenth grade."

"I was attacked," I said. "A man raving about someone he called the Dark Lady—he said she was forcing him to kill me, and he didn't want to do it, but there was nothing he could do about it."

"Coercion is not mind control."

"This was not coercion."

"Is that another hunch?"

"He tried to drown me!" I shouted. "Just like he or someone else drowned Kathy Schrenk and Crabtree Jones. Maybe it was that woman back there, maybe it was someone else, but something in this town is messing with people's heads."

"And you think it's this 'Dark Lady.' "

"It's obviously the Dark Lady," I said, "and that's obviously . . ." I stopped.

"It's obviously what?"

"I'm sorry," I said, "I just remembered that I'm a prisoner, not a fellow agent."

"Don't be a pill about this."

"You don't want my help anyway," I said, "I never had any formal investigative training."

"Is that what this is? I hurt your pride?"

"Not as much as I apparently hurt yours. Sorry to be so much better at your job than you are."

"You can still tell me what you know."

"In exchange for a lighter sentence?" I asked. "Isn't that how this works?"

"John . . ."

"I've missed the last few seasons of *CSI: Demonhunters*, but I'm pretty sure I get to talk to a lawyer."

"And here we go," he sighed.

"Do you have supernatural lawyers?" I asked. "With supernatural lawyering powers? Maybe a Withered who gave up the ability to tell the truth, and now he can force other people to be truthful on the witness stand—"

"Brooke is doing well," said Mills.

I stopped. "What?"

"Brooke is doing well," he said. "She's in an institution, under twenty-four-hour care, and she has her family, and they're all making headway."

"Why are you telling me this?"

"Because you've gone into smartass mode, and I'm sick of arguing with you," he said. "We're going back to my motel, we're going to rendezvous with the rest of my team, and then we're going home to DC. You'll be debriefed, you'll be arraigned, and you'll be imprisoned—all in private meetings, of course; this is top secret. And Brooke is going to want to see you, and you're probably going to want to see her, but we're not going to let you, and we're not even going to tell anyone we found you. So, I'm telling you now, as the one beacon of light in this whole disgusting mess, that Brooke is doing well. The therapy is working, and the meds as well, and she'll be okay. It'll be a slow road, but it'll happen."

I looked out the window, all the fight gone out of me. "Thank you."

"You made the right decision to bring her home," said Mills. "Whatever else you've done, you did that right."

I nodded. The adrenaline drained away, and I felt empty and exhausted again. I closed my eyes. "What about . . ." I stopped myself. I'd almost said "Marci," but I knew what the answer would be. If Brooke was making headway in her therapy, that meant her other personalities were going away. Marci was disappearing, day by day and pill by pill, like a sandstone boulder at the edge of the sea.

"What about who?" he asked.

"Boy Dog," I said instead. "You said you'd take care of him."

"And I have. He's in a kennel, waiting for you to come back."

"They won't let me see him."

Mills drove in silence for a moment before answering. "No, they won't."

It was full dark now, and Lewisville glowed like an ember on the far side of the low desert hills, lighting the sky long before we could see the city itself. I watched the streetlights appear one by one as we rounded the final turn, the small city unfolding like a pocket of stars. We drove through the streets, to a side of town I didn't know well, and pulled into the parking lot of something called the Moonbeam Motel.

Mills stopped the car in the middle of the parking lot—not parking but just . . . stopping.

"Mills?"

He was staring at something, his eyes narrowed and suspicious; I followed his sight line and saw one of the ground floor doors hanging open. Was that his room? Or was something else the problem?

He kept the car in drive, not even engaging the parking brake, and pulled out his cell phone. He held it to his ear, but shook his head.

"He's not picking up."

"Who?" I asked.

"Hang on." He ended the call and tapped in another number, and held the phone to his ear again. I looked out the window, not at the open door but at everything else. Most of the area was lit up, but parts of the periphery were cloaked in shadow. I thought I saw a figure by the fence, but it might have just been a tree branch moving in the wind.

"Hey, Sutton?" asked Mills into his phone. "Do you know where Murray is? He's not answering his phone."

The car was stopped. I wasn't even buckled.

I saw movement in the shadows again; definitely a person. Whoever it was, was swaying back and forth, so much like the homeless woman had been swaying by the canal that I couldn't help but wonder, just for a second, if it was her. But it couldn't be; we'd traveled too fast.

"The door to my room is hanging open," said Mills into the phone. "It's probably just a mistake, like the house-keeper forgot to pull it closed after she was done, but it's tripping my Spidey-sense, and I can't get hold of Murray, and this whole thing is freaking me out."

I opened the car door, and Mills shouted into the phone.

"Now John's leaving—John! Come back here! Sutton, get over here, he's getting away!"

Mills revved the engine, jerking the SUV forward, but I jumped out and managed to land without losing my balance. He swore again, slamming on the brakes and throwing the vehicle into park. I walked toward the figure in the shadows, and I could hear whoever it was in the gaps between Mills's angry shouts behind me; the figure was muttering something, over and over:

"Stay here. Stay here."

Mills grabbed me from behind, and I felt a cold metal handcuff slam down onto my wrist. "I said stay in the car!"

"Shh." I didn't pull away from him, just put my free hand to my lips, and then pointed at the swaying, muttering man.

"He's a junkie," said Mills.

"Listen," I whispered.

"Stay here," the man repeated. "Stay here. The Dark Lady says to stay here."

Mills had his stun gun out before I even knew he was reaching for it. "What's going on here?" he whispered.

"I have no idea," I whispered back.

"Is that the man who attacked you?"

I crept forward, pulling on the handcuff around my right wrist; Mills kept a firm grip on it, but let me lead. I drew closer and recognized the mysterious figure's coat. I nodded, signaling Mills, and then raised my voice just enough to carry.

"Simon Watts?"

The man in the shadows looked up.

"Simon Watts?" I asked. "Can you tell me what happened here?"

"I don't have to talk to you," he said, once again rocking back and forth. "I don't want to talk to you."

"Who is the Dark Lady?" I asked.

Watts shook his head. "Everyone."

Mills grunted, then called out a question of his own: "What did the Dark Lady tell you to do?"

"Stay here."

"I mean before that," said Mills. "What did you do in my motel room?"

"Nothing nothing nothing nothing nothing nothing—"

I took another step forward. "Simon," I said. "Do you recognize me?"

He turned toward us again, leaning forward to get a closer look. He studied my face, and then his eyes opened wide, and then he screamed at the top of his lungs.

Mills fired his Taser, and Watts dropped to the ground, twitching.

"I'm going to need my handcuffs back now," said Mills,

but he didn't actually take them from me. We stared at the body for a moment before he spoke again. "Are you going to run away from me, John?"

"You know me so well." I said, "You tell me."

"An ancient supernatural monster forced this man to do something to my room," said Mills. "You want to see what it was as much as I do. So no, you won't."

I stared at him, then looked at Watts's unconscious body. After a moment, I looked back toward the row of motel doors.

"I reserve the right to run away later."

"And I reserve the right to shoot you when you do."

I nodded and reached out my hand. "Allies until then."

"Don't put it that way," said Mills. "It makes me sound stupid."

"That ship has sailed."

He frowned but shook my hand and holstered his stun gun. He took the cuff off my wrist and put it around Simon's, and then we dragged his unconscious body to the fence and cuffed him to a thick metal post. Once he was secure, Mills drew his real gun.

"Stay behind me," he whispered, and I dropped back half a step as we walked carefully toward the open motel room. We could smell the blood before we even reached the door.

Mills pushed the door open with one hand, keeping his gun up and ready in the other, but then we saw the inside of the room and all formality disappeared.

"Agent Fletcher Murray," Mills whispered.

The body of a black-suited man was laid out on the floor of the room, surrounded by a pool of blood that soaked into the carpet and filled the air with a thick, noxious aroma. The man's chest had been cut open, just like the *Y* incision of an autopsy corpse, with the sternum cracked and the ribs folded out like an old cathedral triptych. The arms had been severed at the shoulders and stuck into the chest cavity, wedged between the organs so that they stood upright and seemed to be reaching toward the ceiling. Even the fingers were carefully arranged, frozen in rigor mortis as if they were trying to catch hold of something distant and ephemeral. The man's shoes were off, and something glimmered wetly against the soles of his feet. I moved to get a better view and saw that it was the man's eyeballs, removed from his head and fastened somehow to the tender skin in the arches above his heels.

"What does it mean?" asked Mills.

"It means the Dark Lady's not playing around anymore," I said.

"Of course," said Mills, "but look at it. It *means* something. It's not just a message, it's . . . art. Even the blood pool on the carpet looks shaped."

I knew what he meant. The body seemed to be . . . written, almost, as if we were reading an ancient glyph in a language we hadn't even realized we knew. I felt like I could almost catch the meaning of it, right at the borders of my understanding. Right at the tip of my tongue.

"There's something in his mouth," I said.

"Yeah," said Mills. Neither of us could see it, but we knew it was there. He reached out carefully, holding onto the nearby bed to keep himself from falling forward and disturbing the scene, and reached a fingertip past the dead man's teeth. He hooked his finger, frowned, and pulled out a small metal ring. "It's from the shower curtain," he said.

"Is there something in the shower?" I wondered.

"No," he said, "it's the shape that's important. A circle. A cycle. A . . . ring, a bracelet, a pit, a hole, a portal, an eye. A wheel."

"An empty plate," I said. "An empty egg. An empty . . . everything. The end of life."

"Circles have no end," said Mills.

I nodded, as if everything were more clear than it had ever been before. "Then the killing will go on forever."

CHAPTER 14

Keeping the crime scene clear was the hardest part— they didn't just need the room analyzed, they needed the corner of the parking lot where we'd left Simon Watts, and all the space in between. Mills and another agent named Rebecca Sutton were working with the local police to collect as much evidence as they could, but guests and tenants kept poking their heads out of the other motel rooms, asking what was going on and were they allowed to leave and who had died and were they in danger and a million other questions. If the police didn't get to them fast enough they just walked out, right past the crime-scene tape, demanding to know if they were under arrest.

Mills and Sutton set the local cops to interviewing them as quickly as possible, getting their IDs and statements on record, while the two agents talked to the motel manager, trying to get contact info for any guests that weren't in their rooms. I, meanwhile, was unceremoniously hand-cuffed to a pipe in Agent Sutton's bathroom. I would have been offended, after promising Mills I wasn't going to run away, but once again he knew me too well. I'd been lying through my teeth.

The pipe I was chained to ran up through the floor and into the bathroom sink, and it was solid enough that I eventually gave up trying to move or break it. Instead I took stock of my situation, studying as much of the room as I could see. I wasn't actually in the bathroom, per se, just next to it—the motel room had a tiny tiled room with a toilet and a shower next to a kind of alcove with a sink and a mirror. Next to that was a small, doorless closet, which led out into the main room. If I stretched as far as possible I could just peek around the corner of the wall to see a small desk, a dresser with a flat-screen TV, and beyond that, the door and a curtained window. There were two beds as well, but I couldn't see more than an inch of each. I knew from when I'd been led in that Agent Sutton had laid out her suitcase on one of the beds, apparently preferring that to putting any clothes in the dresser.

The sink and bathroom, on the other hand, had a few resources I might be able to use. Sutton had cleared out her personal belongings, including a safety razor—I don't know what they thought I was going to do with a safety razor, but they'd kind of made a point of it, so whatever. Her toothbrush, had she left it, might have been a lot more useful: I might have been able to file it down or break it in half to create a sharp point, not so much to stab someone as to try to pick the lock on the handcuffs. I doubt either would have worked, as I'm not exactly a master thief. I really need to learn how to pick a lock.

Of the objects they did not take away from me, there was little I could use. I had two plastic cups, individually wrapped in thin plastic bags. I had travel-size bottles of shampoo and conditioner, and a small bar of white soap. I had an empty black garbage can, about the size of a fast-food bag; it was pretty flimsy plastic and probably wouldn't work well as a weapon, but you never knew. Maybe I could snap that into usable, bladelike pieces? Maybe, but I didn't know how that would help me. Unless I planned to straight-up murder both agents—and somehow managed to kill the first one without alerting the second—hurting them in any way would only make my life harder, not easier. And I didn't want to kill them, anyway. They were only doing what they thought was right.

What did I want? I could try to leave Lewisville again, but where would I go? More importantly, I didn't think I wanted to leave anymore. Yes, I'd decided to leave before, but then Mills had found me and told me that he'd *known* I would run, and I didn't like that. It made me feel dirty, to think that I had a reputation for running away from problems. Sure, I was running from the FBI and half a dozen other agencies and groups that wanted me, but I didn't think of myself as a runner. I fixed things, didn't I? I made things better, no matter how much it hurt me in the process. And yet here I was, the guy who runs away from stuff. I didn't want to be the guy who runs away from stuff.

But I didn't exactly want to be the guy who lives forever in top-secret government custody, either. There had to be a middle ground. "The guy who slips away from the feds but sticks around to stop the Withered" felt like a good thing to be, but I had no idea how to actually pull it off. I didn't even know where the Dark Lady was, let alone how to kill her. And who knew how many other Withered she'd managed to gather. Assu couldn't be the only one.

Thinking about other Withered reminded me of the feral woman out in the desert, and at that thought my arm seemed to throb again, and I realized I'd never cleaned the wounds. Soap and water were the only things I had, but in this case that was exactly what I needed. I ran the tap until it was just shy of being too hot to touch, and then stuck my right arm in it and winced at the pain. My left arm, cuffed to the pipe, was too far to reach, but I eventually managed to wash the long, bloody scratches on both arms by soaking the one and then crouching so I could rub both arms together. It took a while, and I got pretty soaked, but at least I was reasonably certain I wasn't going to get an infection. I turned off the water and sat on the floor, blowing out a long, exhausted sigh, and watched a cockroach scuttle across the linoleum in front of me. Okay, so maybe I still wasn't super clean. At least I felt a little more clearheaded.

I didn't squish the cockroach; most people would have, but I had a rule. No harming living things, even if those living things were roaches. Sorry if that's gross. We all do what we must to survive.

I stretched myself out to full length again, looking into the main room, hoping I'd see something I missed. The desk had a phone, but it was a few feet out of reach, and who would I call, anyway? The police were already here, and they weren't on my side, and I didn't know anybody else's phone number. Maybe if I could reach the lamp I could use that as a weapon, but again: what would be the point? I needed to escape, not hurt anyone. I looked at the rest of the items on the desk: a little binder with hotel info; a plastic card explaining how to use the pay-per-view; a notebook and a pen; a coffee maker—

—wait. A pen. The first thing I'd seen that I might be able to use to pick the lock on my handcuffs. But the desk was still out of reach. I stretched again, reaching my arm as far as I could, grinding my face into the wall to gain even one more inch of distance, but it didn't work. My arm wasn't long enough . . . but my leg was. I looked around for the cockroach, didn't see it anywhere, and laid down on the ground, stretching my legs toward the desk.

I was just able to hook my foot around the nearest table leg, and pulled it toward me, praying that it wasn't nailed down or stuck to the wall. It came about a foot toward me until something stopped it—probably the cord from the phone or the lamp or the coffee maker, or maybe even all three. I managed to get both of my feet around it now, locking it between my ankles, and pulled it toward me with all of my strength. It gave abruptly, flying toward me as whatever had been holding it back suddenly broke or came loose; the lamp fell backwards off the far side, crashing against the floor and shattering the bulb.

I had to be fast. I climbed to my feet, grabbed the pen off the desk, and began picking it apart to get at the useful bits inside. It was a clicky pen, which meant it had a spring and various little plastic pieces; the spring was too soft to work, and the plastic too thick or too short. I stared at all the pieces for a second, then dropped the outer casing on the floor and stomped on it, over and over, until I managed to break it. It came apart in jagged, pen-length shards, and with my teeth and fingernails I managed to carve one of these down into a shape slim and pointy enough to fit into the keyhole on the cuffs. I probed the lock carefully, trying to feel it out, wishing I knew more about it. People in movies picked handcuff locks all the time—was it really possible or was that just a Hollywood thing? I felt resistance in several places, but couldn't get any of the inner mechanisms to move.

The motel room door rattled; someone was coming in.

I shoved my makeshift lock pick into the waistband of my pants and started fiddling with the broken pen bits instead; there was no way to hide what I'd done, and whoever was coming in would obviously take away my tools, but if I focused on the wrong tools maybe they would, too.

Agent Mills was talking as he came into the room:

". . . call headquarters again and request—oh, for crying out loud. John? What the hell are you doing?"

"Don't come back here," I said calmly, "it's a surprise."

One of the agents pulled the desk away from the entrance to my alcove, and then Sutton stepped around with her gun aimed straight for my center of mass. "Drop it."

"I just said don't come back here," I told her. "At least Mills listens to me."

"He's trying to pick the lock with a pen case," said Sutton loudly, and then she motioned toward me with the gun. "I said drop it!"

"Put it down, John," said Mills from around the corner; the entry was too small for both of them to stand in. "You can't pick handcuffs with a pen case."

I kept working on the lock, though the fragment in my hand was too big to actually accomplish anything. "She can't shoot me, I'm too important."

"Ugh," said Sutton, "I hate him already."

"Use your Taser," said Mills. Sutton smiled, holstered her weapon, and pulled out her stun gun instead.

I stopped working. "Are you really going to tase me?"

"Are you really going to let me?"

I raised an eyebrow. "Let you or make you?"

"It's definitely 'let,'" said Sutton. "I'm in a really pissy mood, and I would absolutely love to pull this trigger."

I paused, then put up my hands. "What is it with you guys and stun guns?"

"Good choice," she said. "Now put all those pen pieces in the garbage can and, while you're at it, all that stuff on the counter, too. Then hand the can to me."

I scraped up the broken pen bits, feeling the hidden fragment bite into my waist as I moved, and put them in the garbage can, then stood up and dropped in the plastic cups as well. I put my hand over the soap and stopped, looking back at her with a question: "Can I keep the soap?"

"You can't keep anything you actually want," said Sutton.

"I hate soap."

"Put it in the can."

I rolled my eyes. "You feds get so uptight when one of your friends is gruesomely murdered, geez." I dropped the soap in the can, made a big show about looking for anything else, and then handed the whole thing to her. She took it carefully, keeping the stun gun trained on me with her other hand. I held up my hands to show her I had nothing left, and she shook her head. Whatever patience she had left, I'd worn it out.

Why did I always do that?

"You can't pick handcuffs with a pen anyway," said Mills. "You need a bobby pin."

"Hey, can I borrow a bobby pin?"

"Can I shock him?" asked Sutton.

"Just ignore him," said Mills. "He's just trying to get under your skin."

"Please don't say it that way," said Sutton.

"Sorry," said Mills, "I wasn't thinking."

Sutton walked out of my field of view, and I thought about the dead agent just a few doors down, in the other room. I softened my voice. "Did you know him very well?"

"Don't talk," said Sutton.

"Agent Murray," I said. "I'm very sorry. He seemed . . . well I guess I never met him. But I'm sure he was . . . nice?"

"Is this you being sensitive?" asked Mills.

I smiled, though no one could see me. "Yeah, I kind of suck at it."

"Why are we talking to him?" asked Sutton.

"Because he's been here longer than we have," said Mills, "and he's really kind of terrifyingly good at our job."

"How good?" asked Sutton.

"According to the timeline I've pieced together," said Mills, "he got into town about the same time we did. And while we piddled around and got some clues and whatever, he found and killed a Withered, all on his own."

Sutton whistled.

I couldn't help but smile again, even if it wasn't entirely true.

I heard them sit—a creaking chair and a settling bed—so I pulled out my hidden lock pick and started working again, as quietly as I could. "I'm sorry about your friend," I said. "Are you going to let me go so I can stop anyone else from being killed along with him?"

"Agent Fletcher Murray was a friend of ours," said Mills. "I only met him a few weeks ago, but Sutton's known him for much longer. He was a good agent, and a good man."

"So, let me go," I said again.

"What can you tell us about the Dark Lady?" asked Mills.

I sighed. "I take it that's a no."

"Sorry," said Mills.

"Then why should I help you, if I'm just going to get locked up?" I said. "Shouldn't I get something out of it?"

"You get the knowledge that the killer is stopped," said Sutton. "If the profile he wrote up on you is correct, that'll be enough."

I dug into a new area of the lock, feeling carefully to see if it worked. "Oh, Mills, you wrote a profile on me? That's sweet."

"Who's Mills?" asked Sutton.

"That's what he calls me," said Mills.

I stopped, looked up, then shook my head. "I *knew* you

gave me a fake name," I said. "Agent Sutton, what's his real one?"

"Why'd you give him a fake name?" asked Sutton.

"Just messing with him," said Mills.

"You're both idiots," said Sutton. "We have an actual adult job here, do you realize that?"

"Let me guess," I said. "You're . . . Max Grit. Wally Washington. Jehoshaphat . . . Hamsterlicker."

"Fletcher is dead!" shouted Sutton. "Will someone please start taking this seriously?"

"My name is Sam," said Mills. The room went silent. "Sam Harris. I didn't want him to know because that's his father's name."

I felt my face go inert.

"John used to call himself the Son of Sam," said Mills—or Harris, I guess. "It wasn't a big thing, it's not like he was trying to emulate David Berkowitz or anything, he just . . . he had that connection to his father. And it's virtually the only connection he has. And names have power, so I figured it was best to just leave mine out of this."

"They don't have power over me," I said, but it was only a whisper. It was shocking to me—embarrassing to me—how profoundly just the mention of my father could affect me. I hadn't seen him in years, so why did this bother me so much?

Sometimes I think the only way I'll ever have peace is to just find my father and kill him.

"You should have told me you gave him a fake name," said Sutton.

"I know," said Harris, "but I didn't want to make a big deal of it."

I got back to work with my plastic lock pick.

"John," he said, "you can call me whatever you want."

"I'm good," I said.

"You ready to talk?"

"I said I'm good," I repeated. It well after midnight and I still hadn't slept, but I didn't want to. I hadn't been able to solve this on my own, but I always worked better with someone to bounce ideas off of. Max or Marci or Brooke. If I could get them talking and figure this out, maybe I could get the info I needed and then slip out when no one was looking. I took a breath. "Ask your questions."

"We want to know about the Dark Lady," said Sutton. "The man in the parking lot, Simon Watts, kept talking about her. It was practically all he could say."

"He didn't kill your friend," I said.

"Oh no?" asked Sutton. "And how do you know that?"

"He wasn't bloody," I said. "Anyone who did that much damage to someone would be covered with blood, but he didn't have a drop on him."

"He had blood on his shoes," said Agent Harris. "The rest could have been caught by a smock or a jumpsuit."

"Did you find one?" I asked. "I assume you've checked his car and the garbage and everywhere else?"

"We haven't found it yet," said Sutton, "but that doesn't mean we never will, and that doesn't mean he's innocent."

"Simon Watts tried to drown me a few days ago," I said. "He may have also drowned Kathy Schrenk. This kind of ritualized corpse is not his MO, and it's not the Dark Lady's."

"So, she told him to stay here to throw us off," said Agent Harris.

"He's definitely some kind of a message," I said. "It just depends on what she knows about who's chasing her."

"Well, we know about the Withered," said Sutton.

"Yes," I said, still probing at the cuffs, "but does *she* know that you know? If she thinks you know nothing, then she's probably trying to hand you an open-and-shut case: blood on his shoes, acting deranged, *boom*. Another visionary killer locked up, and you all go on your way, and she carries on unmolested."

"But what are the odds of that?" asked Sutton. "It's more likely that she knows everything."

"Everything, everything?" I asked. I found a part of the lock that seemed to move when I levered the shard of pen against it and tested it cautiously. "If she knows about everything, then this is a declaration of war. She can't be handing us a suspect because she knows that we know that it can't actually be either of the obvious suspects: it's not Watts and it's not the Dark Lady herself."

"How do we know it's not the Dark Lady?" asked Agent Harris.

"Because you have me," I said. "And I know how she and her . . . thralls, or whatever . . . actually function. Like I told you—they came after me once already. So, because I am here, I can tell you what I know, and she wouldn't bother trying to misdirect us after that. Which means she's calling us out."

"Like Rack did in Fort Bruce," said Sutton. "Find the investigators and target them directly."

"That's why I asked for backup," said Agent Harris. "We need all the help we can get."

"No we don't," I said. The mechanism in the lock felt like it would probably work—all I had to do was push on it and it would pop open. Which would probably make an audible click, so I had to wait for the right time. I kept the plastic lock pick in exactly the right place, waiting, and kept talking. "You're not thinking this through. That was the scenario where we assume she knows everything, but I don't think she does. I don't think she knows you have me."

"Come on," said Agent Harris, "how could she not know that?"

"Assume she's done her homework," I said. "She knows about Rack and Fort Bruce. She obviously knows that I exist because she sent Watts to drown me. And she definitely knows about you because A) the FBI's been hunting the Withered for decades and B) you've been asking about me all over town. If she has even one mind-controlled thrall on the police force, she knows that you're here and that—this is the key—you and I are not working together. All she saw today was you looking for me and me leaving town. And by the time we got together Agent Murray was already dead. Even if that homeless woman in the desert is one of her thralls and is somehow reporting back to her, a murder like that takes a long time, and whatever message the Dark Lady was trying to send to us was already in place."

"Yeah," said Sutton, "I can see where you're going with this. If the Dark Lady didn't know we had access to your information, then leaving Watts here to misdirect us is the most plausible scenario. He tells us he did it on her orders, and we have no reason to doubt him. Which means she's trying to make it look like she did it, which . . . means she probably didn't. What?"

"So there's another Withered," said Agent Harris. "The Dark Lady is covering for someone else."

"Exactly," I said. "But why? Why try to hide that there's another Withered in Lewisville?"

"Because concealing information is always valuable," said Sutton. "Why did Jehoshaphat Hamsterlicker here try to hide his real name from you? Deception is valuable for its own sake, especially in a war."

"First," I said, "I love you. Second, I don't think it's that easy. And even if it is, we shouldn't be content with an easy answer. Yes, she's gathering an army, but is she ready to start a war? The only other Withered we know for sure she brought here was Assu, the fire guy, and he's dead. This . . .

this almost feels like Rain's trying to throw us off while she gets some more pieces in place."

"Rain?" asked Agent Harris.

"The Dark Lady," I said. "That's her name, or at least a name she's known by."

"Why would she try to throw us off by painting a target on herself?" asked Sutton. "There's no way."

"But she did," I said. "And we have to consider that. Profiling a killer isn't about denying what doesn't make sense, it's about finding the circumstances where the parts that don't make sense actually do." I paused. "What if the other Withered she's covering for was not acting under her orders?"

Agent Harris grunted.

I nodded, though they couldn't see me. This made sense. "If she really wanted us to think this was her, she would have tried to make it look like one of the others; like a drowning. That's what brought you to Lewisville in the first place. But she didn't, which might mean that the killing was not sanctioned, just like Minaker wasn't sanctioned. It was another Withered, acting without oversight, drawing undue attention where it shouldn't be drawn. She had to do something to throw us off, and Simon Watts was a half-measure—the best she could do under the circumstances. So, there's an uncontrolled Withered in the mix, and that is very, very not good."

"You'd rather have them working together?" asked Agent Harris.

"The Dark Lady is gathering an army," I said. "Two Withered working together would be frightening, I'll grant you, but who knows how many we're going to get by the time she's done. And if she can't control them, who knows what's going to happen. Assu came because she called him, but he wasn't in any hurry to buckle down and start taking orders. There could be dozens more, all in one place, and all just as uncontrolled and dangerous as whoever killed Agent Murray."

"So what else do you know about her?" asked Sutton. "All we're doing is scaring ourselves—we need solid info that we can actually act on."

I nodded again. "Her name is Rain, like I said. 'Run from Rain.'"

"Run from Rain," said Agent Harris.

I looked up. "You've heard that before?"

"What?" he said. "No, I was . . . just thinking about something else. We've got the old transcripts from Elijah Sexton, the Withered you questioned in Fort Bruce, and on one occasion, talking about Rack, he grouped him in with another Withered named Ren. Rack and Ren."

"Wrack and Ruin," said Sutton.

I froze, terrified by the implications that my brain was slowly working through. "We need to get out of here."

"We can't leave," said Agent Harris.

"What do you know?" asked Sutton.

I stood up. "Our historian in Fort Bruce, Nathan, he theorized that Rack was an original name—not a title, like some of the Withered used, but the old, old, ten thousand-year-old name that Rack had had back when he was still human."

"Still human?" asked Sutton.

"They started as humans and gave something up to become Withered," I explained. "We still don't know how they did it, but Nathan's theory is that Rack as a proper name eventually became the proto-Indo-European word for king. Rex and rey and who knows how many others. That he was so powerful so long ago that our word for a ruler is literally just his name. And I was so distracted by Rain meaning 'rain' that it never occurred to me it might mean 'queen.'"

"Reina," said Sutton. "Regina. Damn it all to hell, Sam, this isn't just a Withered—it's the Withered queen."

"We can't leave," said Agent Harris.

"The soldiers are still a few hours out," said Sutton. "I'm going to call them off. If there's a mind-controlling demon queen in town, the last thing we want are a bunch of guys with guns."

"Thank you," I said. "Did I tell you that I love you? You're officially the smartest FBI agent I have ever worked with."

"I don't want to," said Agent Harris.

"You don't want to call them off?" asked Sutton. "Are you kidding?"

I stretched out to try to look around the corner. "You didn't call them off in Dillon and look what happened."

"I don't want to," he said again.

"Agent Harris?" said Sutton. "Sam, are you all right?"

My heart skipped a beat. If he didn't look all right, and he was saying the things he was saying . . .

"I don't want to hurt you," he said. "But the Dark Lady says I have to."

"Sam!" shouted Sutton.

And then someone fired a gun.

CHAPTER 15

I dropped to the floor, covering my head, barely half a second before the wall behind me exploded in a shower of splinters and drywall dust. My ears rang, and I was dimly aware of more gunshots—I couldn't hear them because I was still deafened from the first one, but I could feel them, like deep, distant thuds that seemed to rattle my bones. I tried to move toward the bathroom, thinking the tub might give me better cover, but I was still cuffed to the pipe—and I'd dropped my lock pick. I looked around wildly, scattering the debris from the gunshots, flicking aside another cockroach that I hadn't even seen was there. I found the plastic fragment just as the wall next to me shook with another impact, but it wasn't a gun this time. The two agents were grappling.

I shoved the pick into the handcuff lock, trying desperately to find the tiny mechanism I'd found before. Where was it? The wall shook again, dislodging more plaster, and I could see flashes of movement through the bullet holes. My hearing came back slowly, and bit by bit the physical hits and thuds became audible as well—a crack as a body hit the wall. A grunt as someone absorbed a blow. A high-pitched cry as Sutton either gave or received a powerful punch. Where was the catch in the lock? I'd found it before. I had to find it again or—

"I don't want to hurt you!" shouted Harris. "Please stop me!"

Somebody grabbed the phone off the desk—I didn't see who, just a hand in a suit coat sleeve that could have been either one. The hand yanked the phone away faster than I could discern any details, ripping the cord out the wall, and I heard it ring suddenly—not a long, controlled trill from an incoming call, but a short metallic tone as some internal piece of metal rebounded off a solid surface. Behind the ring was a crunch, and then a thud as a body fell to the floor.

"I didn't want to do it," said Harris. He was crying. "Please don't make me do it."

Footsteps. A long, gravelly scrape as he dragged a chair across the floor. He was coming for me now. The table moved, clearing his final path to come around the corner.

And the handcuff sprung open.

I leaped to my feet, stumbling backward into the bath-room. Was he getting his gun? Did he have any bullets left? His hand came around the corner, holding the black telephone like a club, and I kicked the door closed to buy myself time. They'd taken everything, right down to the flimsy plastic garbage can . . . but they'd forgotten one thing. I jumped up and grabbed the rod for the shower curtain, hanging all my weight on it; it was barely at-tached, one more chance for the motel to pinch another penny, and it snapped down from its place on the wall just as Harris kicked the door open. I swung the shower rod with all my might, trailing the curtain like a flag, and caught him in the side of the head before he'd even come into the room. The force slammed his skull against the door frame, and he dropped to the floor like a stone.

I stood in the bathtub, my ears still ringing, my heart still pounding. Sam Harris. I wanted to hit him again, to feel that one perfect moment of crunch as the metal broke the bone—no, I wanted to stab him. It was always my fa-vorite, so sharp and bloody and perfect—

No.

I didn't want to do any of it.

I wasn't out of control, and I wasn't under Rain's con-trol, either. I was me. And I was in charge.

I dropped the rod and it clattered to the ground in a billow of beige plastic sheeting. I stared at the body and swallowed. Was he alive? Was Sutton? What should I do?

I could hear shouting in the distance; someone had heard the fighting, or more likely the gunshots. Were the cops still here? What would they think when they found me here, the only one left standing?

I stepped out of the tub and over Agent Harris's body. His legs trailed out past the sink, and on a sudden impulse I bent down and slapped the open handcuff around his ankle. He wasn't evil, but if Rain had gotten her hooks in him, I couldn't have him following me. I stood up, and then realized I hadn't even stopped to check his pulse—I was so concerned about stopping the bad guy, I hadn't thought to save the good guy. Even when it was the same person. I went back and put my fingers on his neck. His heart was beating. I moved out of the alcove and into the other room, finding Agent Sutton slumped along the floor and pausing to check her pulse as well. She was alive, but the bump on her head from the telephone was already as big as a golf ball. Both of their guns were on the floor as well, but I didn't know how to check if they still had bullets. I kicked them under the bed and left Sutton with her stun gun. If she woke up before Harris did, she'd need it.

I grabbed Agent Harris's keys from the top of the dresser and opened the door. If anyone was watching, they were too far out in the dark for me to see; everyone else was probably hiding from the gunshots, and there were no police in sight. They'd left from their first investigation here tonight and hadn't had time to respond to this new one yet. I jogged across the parking lot, climbed into Harris's SUV, and drove away.

The roads were dark and the sky was lit with streetlights and neon. I stopped at the first traffic light, still trying to catch my breath. What should I do? I had the means to leave again, and to get so much farther than before; they'd track the SUV, but I could abandon it in another town, or, better yet, give it to someone and head off in a different direction. That could throw them off for days.

But the problem was here. And I didn't want to feel again the way I'd felt when Mills—when Harris—had found me. Like I'd abandoned the people who needed my help. The light turned green, but I didn't move forward. The problem was here. Jasmyn had said once that everyone was worth saving.

So, I guess I had to save them.

I took my foot off the brake and turned the wheel to the left. I knew Jasmyn's address—I wouldn't be much of a paranoid obsessive if I didn't—and it was just a few miles away. If Lewisville really was filling up with Withered, and if Harris really had called for reinforcements, this town was about to be another war zone, maybe even worse than Fort Bruce. I still didn't know where Rain was, but I knew where my friends were, Jasmyn and Margo and Harold. I could help them, at least, maybe get them out of town before the real trouble started. I checked the mirrors compulsively as I drove, expecting at any moment to see lights and hear sirens behind me, but nothing came. I pulled into the parking lot of Jasmyn's apartment complex and looked at the clock: 3:38 A.M. I left the SUV running as I jogged up a flight of old cement stairs to Jasmyn's apartment, and I knocked on her door.

And waited.

I knocked again. Could she even hear me? Maybe she slept with earplugs or something, or a white-noise machine to drown out ambient sound. I pounded on the door harder and counted to ten as slowly as I dared, then pounded again and shouted.

"Jasmyn! Wake up!"

"Shut up out there, it's the middle of the night!" The voice had come from another building across the parking lot. I ignored it and banged on the door again.

"Jasmyn!"

"Robert?"

I heard a bolt scrape in the door frame, and then the door opened about two inches, stopped by the chain. A bleary-eyed face appeared in the crack of light, but it wasn't Jasmyn.

"Al!sha?"

"Robert, it's the middle of the night. What are you doing here?"

"You need to get out of here," I said. "You and Jasmyn both. Is she awake?"

"She's not here, she said she had something to do."

Crap. "Do you know where she went?"

"Robert," she said, "are you okay? Is Jasmyn okay?"

"Do you know where she went?"

"She went to work," said Al!sha. "It was like midnight or something. I don't know why."

"Okay," I said, "I'll go there. Do you have a car?"

"You can't have my car."

"I don't want your car, I want you to get in it and drive away. Anywhere you can go that's not in Lewisville—family, friends, whatever, just get out. Will you do that?"

"Why would I do that? What did you do?"

"I haven't done anything," I said, "but somebody's going to. Get out now." I turned and ran back to the SUV. Al!sha called after me once, but only once, and then she closed the door. I didn't know if she believed me or not, but I didn't have time to wait around. If Jasmyn was headed to the mortuary then maybe . . .

Wait.

Jasmyn.

I got into the vehicle and closed the door, then sat there, thinking. Withered were incredibly hard to identify because they usually just looked like normal people—Rack being the obvious exception. But there were two things about the Withered that were usually true:

First. If a Withered could shape shift they could be any-body, but if their powers swung more toward body stealing—and a lot of them did—it was easier to steal teenage bodies. Teenagers were turbulent enough as it was; the foods and the music and the people they liked could change from week to week, or even day to day, so a Withered could step into their life and assume their role without raising a ton of questions. They could do an imperfect impression of the person they were trying to imitate, or even a flat-out terrible impression, and the people in their life would chalk it up to puberty or hormones. So there was that.

Second. If a Withered didn't steal bodies or shape shift at all, that meant they still had their original bodies from ten thousand years ago. Rack had had his, and Assu, and one named Yashodh. And they had all looked distinctly nonwhite. The old valley they sometimes talked about was probably in the Middle East somewhere; Nathan had theorized it might be in Turkey.

I put the SUV in gear and pulled back onto the street.

If Rain was a shape-shifter she'd be impossible to detect, but if she was either other body type, both of them pointed to Jasmyn. A young girl or a Middle Eastern girl. Why hadn't Jasmyn wanted to talk about her past? Because she was a demon queen? And why had Margo taken her in with no prior knowledge or references of any kind? Was Jasmyn controlling her mind?

Rain had attacked me literally the first day I appeared in town. How had she known I was here? I can believe that Rain would know who I was, especially if she'd been working with Rack, but I'd only met a handful of people that day. It had to be one of them.

I didn't want it to be Jasmyn, but it's like I told the

agents: my job wasn't to find the pieces I wanted, it was to find the pieces that were there and then figure out how they fit. And if the puzzle came together into a portrait I didn't like, well, there wasn't anything I could do about that. I didn't get to pick my own reality. And I sure as hell wouldn't have picked this one if I did.

The lights at the mortuary were on. I pulled up to the curb and got out, walking slowly to the front door with my backpack over my shoulder. It sang a little song as I passed the motion sensor, and then Harold stepped out of the door.

"No one's allowed in," he said. His voice was hollow, like he was an empty shell dressed up as a person.

He was already a thrall. Did I dare to get any closer? If she just turned me into a thrall as well, then everything I'd worked for would end—I wouldn't be dead, but I'd never get to make my own choices ever again, and that seemed even worse. My body would be doing whatever the Dark Lady wanted, with my mind just watching, help-less and trapped.

Just like Brooke when Nobody had taken her over.

"I'm here to see Jasmyn," I said. I couldn't run away anymore, and I couldn't let anyone else lose their lives to these monsters. "It's me, Harold. You can let me in."

"She doesn't want you here," said Harold.

I took a step closer. "Does she know it's me? Maybe she told you not to let anyone else in, but I'm okay. She knows me. You know me."

"I'll ask her," he said, and then he just stood there, staring at me dumbly. I waited for several seconds before venturing to ask:

"Are you going to go—"

"She says no," said Harold. "She says she knows it's you, and that your name is John Cleaver, and that she's always known it was you, ever since you got here."

"Okay," I said. I licked my lips, trying to think. She hadn't taken over my mind yet, so maybe I could keep him—or her—talking. "Did she say why?"

"She doesn't have to say why," said Harold. "She's the Dark Lady. She's the beginning and the end."

"And if I come inside anyway?"

"Then I'll kill you."

"But you don't want to," I said. "Just like the others didn't want to. They tried to fight it, but they're not as strong as you are, Harold, you can fi—"

"Of course I want to," he said. "It's all I want in the world."

I stared at him, and then I felt my shoulders sink as the truth set it. Because of course.

"You want what she wants because you're not new," I said. "She's been controlling you for twenty years, and there's nothing of your own will left."

His answer was so soft I almost didn't hear it: "Twenty-five."

"Because Jasmyn's here," I said, "but she's not the Dark Lady."

"Of course not."

I nodded. "Margo is."

"The light that shaped the world," he said. "The mother of darkness."

Of course it was Margo. The absolute authority that the others only orbited.

I couldn't give up yet.

"What is she doing?" I asked.

"Talking."

"To who?"

"To Jasmyn," he said. "And Carol. And Shelley Jones."

So Jasmyn wasn't a thrall, then. They were talking. But what did Margo have to say to Jasmyn at 3:30 in the morning? And to Carol and Shelley? I didn't know why Jasmyn was there, but I could guess about the other two: they were the survivors, left behind after the deaths of their only companions. Rain hadn't been killing lonely people, she'd been making other people lonelier. Sadder. She was destroying the only things that kept them going, and replacing them with pain.

Pain that she could take away.

"She's doing the ritual, isn't she?" I asked. "She's going to make more Withered."

"They are Blessed."

"Then take me in there," I said. "Take me in to the ritual." I took a deep breath, and said it as firmly as I could:

"I want to be a Withered, too."

CHAPTER 16

Harold stood still, his shoulders slumped, his face inert. After a moment he turned toward the door. "Come inside." He opened the door, and I followed him in.

Margo was in her office—not the fancy one, but the backroom office where things got done. Her desk was full but tidy, with papers and folders laid neatly in boxes marked IN and OUT. She sat behind the desk, looking weary but powerful; the face of a woman ready to make impossible choices. Around her, the office was full of people crowded in among the bookshelves and filing cabinets and boxes of old papers stacked high against the wall. Carol and Shelley in their seats, tired and disheveled;

Jasmyn leaning against a bookcase; Mr. Connor, the accountant, standing at solemn attention.

I looked at Mr. Connor, made a handful of quick deductions, then looked at Margo. "I assume he's the body displayer?"

"You were always smarter than I gave you credit for," said Margo. "You found me by accident, but you still found me. Because you put yourself in the right place to have the accident you needed."

"Thanks."

She gave me a weary look. "I assume you're not here for the ritual."

"What ritual?" asked Jasmyn.

"Sorry," I said. "I'm mostly just here to figure out how to kill you."

Margo looked at me a moment, then a sly smile crept into the edges of her mouth. "Good luck."

"So what's your thing?" I asked Mr. Connor, looking away from Margo and brightening my voice. "You gave up . . . I don't know, sculpting? Can you give up a skill? Abandon all sculpting, and then you can only sculpt when you kill a person to do it? You have to admit, that's the dumbest godlike power I think I've ever heard."

"Wait," said Jasmyn, "you know about this? You know what they are?"

"To my ongoing personal sadness, yes," I said. "How much do you know?"

"I know that Margo has no abdomen," said Jasmyn,

and the look in her eyes made it clear that she was still reeling from the shock. "Have you . . . seen it?"

I thought about Rack, whose chest and neck and lower face were completely gone, replaced by a roiling cauldron of ashy black soulstuff. "No," I said. "Though I've seen things like it." If Margo had a similar deformity— something that obviously marked her as supernatural—it made sense that she'd start this particular meeting by showing it off. Jasmyn and the two older women were shocked, but at least they knew this was horribly, inescapably real.

Margo answered my question: "Mr. Connor gave up his imagination."

I gave him an appraising glance. "How did that help you?"

"I can't think of anything new," he said, "but I can remember existing facts with perfect clarity and manipulate them as necessary."

"You sound like an android," I said.

"If that helps you," said Mr. Connor.

"Mr. Connor can't think of anything new *on his own*," said Margo, and her voice was tired and heavy as she said it. "But he can draw inspiration from other people."

I thought about Agent Murray's body, arranged so carefully it seemed like a work of art. "By killing them," I said.

"Inspiration is a physical substance," said Mr. Connor. "Extracting it is an invasive process."

"That's why I like the word 'draw,'" said Margo. "It sounds like he's just being inspired instead of . . . pressing it out, like oil from an olive."

"That is not an exact metaphor—" said Mr. Connor, but Margo cut him off.

"I didn't want him to kill that agent," she said.

Jasmyn and the older women gasped. "You killed someone?" demanded Jasmyn.

"I figured as much," I said, keeping my eyes focused on Margo. The longer I kept her talking, the more opportunity I had to come up with a plan. "You left Simon Watts there to cover for him, but there were too many loose ends."

"I told you you were clever."

"I prefer 'terrifyingly good at what I do,'" I said. "Though I guess the guy who said that is a mindless thrall now."

"I call them children," said Margo.

I shook my head. "You can call them cockatiels if you want, but they're still mindless thralls."

"I don't want to hurt anyone—"

I scoffed. "That'd be a lot easier to believe if you hadn't told one of your cockatiels to drown me in a canal."

"I don't want to hurt anyone," she said again, "but sometimes I have to. Sometimes we all have to. Life isn't easy—"

"That's the worst excuse for murder I've ever heard."

"Will you let me finish a damn thought?" she snapped.

"I'm not doing this because I want my life easy; life is work, and work is hard. And sometimes our decisions are hard. But when the alternative is extinction, you make those hard decisions, and you live with them because the alternative is never living with anything, ever again."

I watched her for a moment, slightly overawed by the power in her voice. Then I spoke again, more softly this time. "That's a much better excuse. But I'm still not sold on the war you're trying to start."

"I don't want a war."

"Then why are you gathering an army?"

"You call Mr. Connor an army?"

"You and Mr. Connor and Assu and who knows how many others—"

"There's only three of us left."

I was struck dumb again, not by her voice, but by the terrifying finality of the words that voice had spoken. Only three left.

"You really are dying," I said. "You really are going extinct."

"You can cheer if you want," she said, throwing her hand out to the side. "You talk about my army, but you started the war, and you've killed and killed and now there's only three of us left in the whole wide world. Three of the grandest and most glorious beings that ever walked the earth, standing around in an old desert town full of rednecks and hippies, meeting at night so we don't get lynched, hiding our names and our faces so we don't get stalked and studied and put down like animals. And then the greatest killer our kind has ever known—and it's a kid, of all things, barely out of training wheels—shows up at my front door and asks me for a job, and I know my time has come. My number's been called. You killed us all, John. The hunter is home from the hill."

Three left, and one of them already gone. Two to go. This is what I'd been working for my entire life.

"Your name is John?" asked Jasmyn.

"She just told you I'm a serial killer," I said, though I didn't take my eyes off of Margo. "And you focus on my name?"

"John Cleaver?" she asked.

"Yeah."

"I looked that name up after you said it before. You knew that FBI agent—" she stopped suddenly, and her face went pale. "Oh no!" She looked at Mr. Connor. "Is that the agent you killed?"

"I killed his companion," said Mr. Connor.

Jasmyn's eyes filled with tears, glistening in the harsh fluorescent light. "That doesn't make it better."

"But you saw it," said Mr. Connor, and he fixed me with a cold, analytical stare. "You saw the muse."

I thought about the displayed, mutilated body again and tried to keep my voice even. "That's a creepy thing to call a corpse."

His eyes seemed to pierce me. "What did it say to you?"

"I . . ." An empty circle. An empty everything. "It said that if we keep fighting, we'll kill each other forever."

Mr. Connor tilted his head to the side. "All death is forever."

"I mean the killing itself will go on forever," I said. "I kill you, Margo kills me, Jasmyn kills Margo, Harold kills Jasmyn, and on and on and on forever." I shook my head. "Except it's not forever, because then you'll be gone. There's only two of you left!" I was practically shaking as I spoke. "Don't you see what this means? We can finally end it!"

"I saw the muse too," said Margo. "I didn't want him to do it, but he did it, and before I posted Watts there to guard it, I looked at it long and hard, because I needed the inspiration as much as anybody. Sometimes I think his muses only tell us what we want to hear, but I needed to hear something. And it told me the time had come."

"For the ritual," I said.

Margo nodded. "We don't end this your way, we end it mine. We don't kill, we create—more lives, more Blessed, more glories upon the earth. Not an empty circle but a full one."

"Don't do this to them," I said.

"Do what?" asked Jasmyn.

"Save you," said Margo. "Take away your pain and put power in its place."

"She wants to make you a monster," I said.

"I want to make you my child," said Margo.

Jasmyn stared at her, then looked at me, then looked back at Margo. "I don't understand."

Margo leaned forward, resting her forearms on the desk. "Mr. Connor and I are ten thousand years old, give or take. And we're not some kind of alien creatures, we're human beings, just like you. Or we were. We found a way to be something more."

"And less," I said.

"More powerful," said Margo. "Less weak. More brave and less scared. More resilient to pain and damage and heartache, and less liable to—"

"Less human," I said.

"We've been queens and kings and gods and goddesses," said Margo. "We've been emperors and pharaohs, and we've been dreams and idols. And all you have to do is give something away, something dark and awful that you don't want, and you give it away of your own free will, and then you become a god."

"They'll never do it," I said. "Maybe ten thousand years ago, but not today."

"People haven't changed," said Margo. "The world's changed, but the people in it are the same as they ever were: they're sad, they're alone, they're scared. What do you never want to be again, honey? Hungry? Vulnerable? Hurt? You were betrayed by your own father—give that up. You were lost and broken and alone—give that up. I can't say exactly what you'll get in return, but you'll get something, and it will change you forever."

"Not all change is good," I said.

The room felt hushed, like the waves had receded out into the ocean, and we sat there waiting for them all to come back. It was Jasmyn who broke the silence.

"Giving things up never helped me before," she said. She paused again, thinking. "I gave up my will when I let other people make choices I didn't like. I gave up my hope, and then I gave up my home and my family and my future. But not one of those was a good decision, and I had to fight to get them back."

"You gave up good things and held on to so many bad ones," said Margo. "What about guilt? I know you feel guilty, even though it wasn't your fault. So give up your guilt."

"And then what?" I asked, and looked at Jasmyn. "You haven't seen the Withered like I have."

"Blessed," said Margo.

"Withered," I insisted. "Cursed and Withered and all dried up, like weeds in the sun. You give up your guilt and then what? You're not complete anymore. We need guilt the same way we need pain—because it reminds us what happened, and it helps us not to do it again. Lose your guilt and you'll forgive your family, and you'll go home and be right back in the same situation without any way to protect yourself. Guilt is our emotional immune system."

"John mythologizes guilt," said Margo, "because it's the only way to justify how much of it he's carrying."

"That doesn't mean I'm wrong."

"And it doesn't mean I am, either," said Margo. "Maybe guilt works for you, and I'm glad that it does, but Jasmyn's different."

"Jasmyn's smarter," I said. "She knows it won't help to give anything up. She already said she never gave up anything."

"Jasmyn's sitting right here," said Jasmyn, "and she can speak for herself." She paused a moment, then shook her head. "Can your ritual take away hate? My therapist taught me to hold on tight to my hope and my future and, yes, even my guilt, or at least part of it, because it helps keep me safe, just like John said. But she always told me to let my hate go." She closed her eyes. "I used to hate my father, and I used to hate my mother for letting him hurt me, and I used to hate my family and my church and my whole neighborhood for looking the other way, and for taking his side, and for calling me the bad one. A temptress or a liar or a troublemaker or a whore. And I used to hate myself, because I believed them. But I let go of it all." She opened her eyes and looked at Margo. "Can I give up my hate?"

Margo nodded, earnest and intense. "Of course you can, honey."

"Of course I can," said Jasmyn, and her face became grim. "And I already did. I don't need to be a monster to do it."

"Yes," I said, clenching my hand into a fist and then pointing a finger solidly at Margo. "You see? I told you she wouldn't do it."

"You're failing to consider all the benefits," said Mr. Connor. "Weigh the costs against the gains: give up your hate, or whatever you decide to part with, and you'll receive not just power, but immortality. I am ten thousand years old. I've read more books that you've ever known existed; I've talked to more people, seen more places, eaten more food, and lived more lives that you can possibly comprehend. I've watched the sun rise over the most distant reaches of the globe, and set again behind cityscapes so bright and alive they replaced the stars. And all you have to do to get that is to give up something you're not even using anyway."

"You've seen those things," I said, "but did you enjoy them?"

"I lost my imagination," said Mr. Connor, "not my pleasure or my peace."

"But when you saw them," I said, "when you saw the oceans and the mountains and the sky—did you think about what was beyond them?"

"I know what is beyond them."

"No daydreams," I said. "No ambitions. You've seen the most glorious sights in the world and they've never inspired you."

"I make my own inspiration."

"And the world is darker because of it," I said. "You've seen a million clouds, but you've never seen a dragon in any of them."

"We're not talking about pictures in the clouds," said Margo. "We're talking about power and immortality."

"I don't want them," said Jasmyn.

"I do," said a frail, old voice. I looked over and saw Shelley Jones, quiet and forgotten in her chair, her walker in front of her like a cold metal cage. Her hands sat folded primly in her lap, shaking slightly from an age-induced tremor. "My Crabtree is dead," she said. "And my baby boy died when he was three years old. I could never have any more after that. Everyone I came from is gone, and no one is coming from me, and all I'm leaving to the world is a ramshackle house in an old junkyard, and no one will ever live there again. Even if they do, they won't remember me. All I have left of life is the fact that I haven't died yet—I'm like a scrub oak, growing from the side of a red-rock cliff, perched where I have no business, twisted and stunted and fighting for every drop of water I can get. I'm not dead, but that's not the same thing as being alive." She closed her rheumy eyes and tears crept down her face, and she raised her trembling hands a few inches off her lap. "Can you take away my pain? It hurts to walk and sit and stand and lay down. It hurts to move my hands and hold a fork and swallow and breathe. Can you take that all away from me?"

"Of course I can," said Margo softly. "That's why I brought you here."

"But it can't be real," said Shelley. "I know it can't be real because it's impossible to be real, and this is all a joke, and I don't know why you're telling it, but any minute now you're going to stop and tell me I have to feel this pain forever."

"It's not a joke," said Margo. She straightened in her chair and then lifted the bottom of her long shirt, exposing her belly—but there was no belly there: her abdomen was a wide, dark cavity, like a cave of obsidian and tar, and pulsing inside of it was the greasy black ash of soulstuff. The heat of it seemed to fill the room. "I can do it," said Margo. "I can take away everything you never wanted to be."

Shelley kept her eyes closed, and her voice was a violent whisper. "Then let's do it."

CHAPTER 17

"Don't do it," I pleaded. "You don't know what you'll become."

"Whole again," said Mr. Connor.

"But what else?" I asked. "Mr. Connor can't imagine it, but I can. Give up your pain and you might become a living sensor for it—I knew a Withered who couldn't feel his own emotions, but he could feel everyone else's and it broke him. Give up your pain and that rest home you live in will become a never-ending nightmare of shared affliction."

"You can't know that for certain," said Mr. Connor, "or I would I know it."

"No we can't," I said. "It might be worse. Maybe you'll lose all physical sensation completely, pain and pleasure and taste and touch. Maybe you'll be driven mad by the simple impossible desire to eat a strawberry just one more time. Maybe you'll have to kill people to absorb their ability to feel, just for a few minutes, like Mr. Connor does with inspiration. Or maybe you won't lose your pain completely and automatically—maybe all you'll gain is the power to shunt that pain off onto other people, making them miserable so you don't have to be. Is that what you want? For other people to suffer the way you have?"

"It never ends," said Shelley, tears forming in her eyes. "Even with pills. This way it would—even if only for a moment."

"But you'd do that to people?" asked Jasmyn. "You'd really give them all your pain like that, and your aches and soreness and torment and anguish?"

"I could find people willing to take it," said Shelley. "How many nurses and doctors and well-meaning neighbors have told me over the years that they'd gladly suffer in my place if they could? I always thought they were just saying that to be polite." Her face grew hard. "If they were just lying, to hell with them."

I growled in frustration. "Think about what you're saying!"

"No," Jasmyn said, and looked at Margo. "Think about what *she's* saying. What she's doing. Did you orchestrate this whole thing?"

"No," said Margo.

"Did you drown Shelley's husband?" asked Jasmyn. "You needed someone sad and hurt and desperate enough to become a monster, and now you have one."

"Honey—" said Margo.

"Did you kill Kathy?" Jasmyn shouted. She stared at Margo, and her eyes welled up with tears. "Did you hurt me, too? If you can make anyone do anything you want, did you make my father—"

"No," said Margo. "Never."

"Prove it," growled Jasmyn.

"I'm trying to help," said Margo. "You think I have to go to all this trouble to find people in pain? Or people willing to sacrifice humanity for power? I can find those people anywhere—I can go out on the streets right now and find a dozen before dawn. I didn't set you up and ruin your life as a part of some evil master plan, just like I didn't warp Shelley's joints and bones, and just like I didn't kill my own friend Kathy. I called you here because you're hurt and I can help you."

"Prove it," said Jasmyn again.

Margo stared at her, then whispered a name into the dark. "Cal Dexter, 2013." She watched Jasmyn, then spoke again. "Leslie Tyler, 2006. Kendra Blaylock, 1999. Luis Palomeque, 1997. Do you want me to go on?"

"People you've killed?" I asked.

"People she's saved," said Jasmyn. "I know some of them—I met Cal over Christmas, and I think Leslie, too.

They're all people she's taken in and given shelter and a job and gotten back on their feet. Just like you and me."

"Mind control?" I asked.

"I didn't control you," said Margo. "Didn't control Jasmyn."

"But you did control Harold," I said. "And Simon Watts, and who knows how many others. Maybe you saved these people, and that's great, but you tried to kill me."

"I thought I had to," said Margo.

"And Kathy?" I demanded. "And Crabtree? You drowned them, too, no matter what you told Jasmyn just now."

"I said you were smart," said Margo, and she shot me a glance from the side of her eye. "That doesn't mean you've figured out everything."

Did she . . . did she not kill them? But then who did? I stood still as a stone, watching her carefully, trying to see what I'd missed. The Dark Lady tried to drown me, and Margo was the Dark Lady. Margo was Rain.

But that didn't mean all the drownings were her.

Three of us left, she'd said, but Assu was already dead. There was another one out there. Rain had sent Watts to kill me for the same reason she'd sent him to the motel: to cover for someone.

"Props on that one," I said, shaking my head. "You got me."

Rain nodded.

"Who's the other one?"

"You'll figure it out."

"My joints are on fire," said Shelley. "Let's get on with this."

"But why?" Jasmyn asked, stopping Shelley with her hand and looking intently at Rain. "If you're some kind of ancient monster, why did you help me? Why help any of us?"

"Because you needed help," said Rain.

"I told her not to," said Mr. Connor.

"Did you control people's minds to do it?" asked Jasmyn. "When I got my partial tuition refunded, was that you messing with the college clerk? When I . . . found my new apartment—was that you, too?"

"Tuition, yes," said Rain. "Apartment, no. I can't do everything for you, or it doesn't work."

"What doesn't work?" demanded Jasmyn. "You said you weren't grooming me for this ritual you keep talking about, so then what were you doing?"

Rain didn't answer.

"She was raising you," I said.

Jasmyn frowned. "Huh?"

"She called the thralls her children," I said, "but I think we're the real ones: the 'wayward ducklings' she keeps taking in. The others are servants, but we're her children. Or at least she wanted us to be." I looked at Rain. "What did you give up? You can control minds and you can make Withered, and I could never figure out the opposite of that. You didn't give up your own mind to control others, and you didn't give up your own control as far as I can tell. But that's the key, isn't it? You keep taking people under your wing; helping them out. That's what you gave up."

"Children," said Rain. She looked into the distance, like she was looking straight into the past, and her thoughts traveled so far back her voice almost seemed to echo across an invisible chasm. "Rack gave up his heart, and Hulla her body, and Kanta his identity. Pta his inspiration. Yashodh his love. I gave up my children."

Jasmyn's face contorted in horror. "Actual children?"

"I was pregnant," said Rain. "Barely more than a month or two—we weren't quite as precise in those days, of course. And it all came down to that: that's where it all started. Everyone else could give up something they hated about themselves, but I had to give something I loved or the ritual wouldn't work, so I lost my child and every child I could ever have, ever again. And not just the biological ones, the emotional ones. I can never have a legacy. I can never have someone who needs me. Cal came to the Christmas party, but he won't come again this year. He has to move on because that's how it works. You'll do the same."

"You found me in a rape-crisis group," said Jasmyn.

"Seemed like a good place to find someone who needed me," said Rain. "And you did for a while, but then you moved away. Pretty soon you'll get another job, and then I'll never see you again."

"That's not supernatural," I said. "That's life. People

move on. People end up alone. Shelley doesn't have any children, either."

"I didn't say that being barren has made me a monster," said Rain, "or being alone, or being unneeded, or anything else. It's the other way around. Being a monster is what made me alone." She shifted in her chair and raised her shirt again, and that deep black pit yawned out of her belly. "I can't have children, but I can have pale, hollow copies of them. Thralls, if you want to call them that, and Blessed. I can't create life, but I can change it. I can save Shelley right now from the pain that is destroying her life, and then I can save Carol, and then I can save Jasmyn and even you, John. I can do it." She was practically pleading now. "We can make the world better."

"It never makes the world better," I said. "You save one life and destroy countless more. You saved Nobody from the imperfect body that she hated, but her imperfections were still there. Her self-doubt, her jealousy, her lack of confidence and satisfaction. You solved a symptom but not the cause, and then she killed a hundred thousand girls trying to find the happiness you couldn't give her."

"I was foolish," said Rain. "I know better now how to take away the right thing."

"My pain isn't a symptom," said Shelley. "Take it away and I'll be me again, whole and normal and perfect."

"You'll be the kind of person who makes a deal with the devil to get what she wants," I said. "There's nothing perfect about it."

"I won't kill anyone," Shelley insisted.

"Of course you will," I told her. "They all do. I don't know how the process works but that's a part of it, right down to the core, because every other Withered has killed people, every time, in every case—even the ones who didn't want to. They're parasites on the world who can never get what they need without taking it from us."

"Just like every human being," said Mr. Connor.

"With one difference," I said. "Humans can stop."

We all stared at each other, watching and thinking, and then Shelley raised herself in agony to her feet. "Enough talk," she said. "Let's get on with it. She's the one with the power here—she doesn't have to listen to you if she doesn't want to."

No, I thought. She doesn't.

And yet she had.

I looked at Rain, and Rain looked at me, and I tried to imagine her as she used to be, back in the ancient valley where all of this had started—a young woman, soon to be a mother, happy and healthy and eager to help everyone around her. So willing to help that she'd damned herself to ten thousand years of loss and pain and regret trying to make other people happy. And then I thought about my own mother, who'd done the same for me for sixteen years—a tiny fraction of some lives, but the entirety of mine.

What did Rain see when she looked at me?

She watched me with ancient eyes, staring and thinking. Eventually she shook her head, lowering her shirt back over the mass of soulstuff.

"No," she said. "I'm sorry, Shelley, I truly am. But John's right. I can't pretend I'm making the world better by putting more Withered in it."

"I'll be benevolent," said Shelley. "I'll use my power for good."

"We all said that in the beginning," said Rain. "But beginnings don't last forever."

Shelley clutched the handles of her walker and her mouth moved, trying for an argument or even a word, but nothing came. She began to cry, and lowered herself in misery to her chair.

I watched Rain, and when my backpack began singing—all three songs at once, loud and cacophonous and shocking—I closed my eyes and shook my head.

"Well, crap," I said.

"What?" asked Jasmyn. "What does that mean? Do you have three cell phones?"

"They're motion sensors," I said. "The FBI is here, and with all their reinforcements. We're surrounded."

"Why crap, then?" asked Jasmyn, rising to her feet. "They can save us, right? They know you're the good guy and those two are the bad guys, and they can take them away or . . . whatever they do, and we're going to be okay. Right? Why crap?"

"Because you were right," I said. "The other day, when that guy burned to death and we thought it was a murder, you said everyone is worth saving. And it sucks, but you were right."

"Why does that suck?"

I opened my eyes and looked at Rain. She looked back, but didn't speak.

"Because everyone means everyone," I said. "And now we have to save the queen of demons."

CHAPTER 18

"I need to think," said Mr. Connor.

"No you don't," I said quickly, stepping toward him in the cramped office. "We're trying to save you two, and I know how you think, so there's no thinking allowed, okay? The last thing that strike team is going to want to see when they get in here is one of our bodies tastefully redecorated on the floor here."

"They'll shoot us," said Carol.

"They'll be a lot less likely to if you're lying down," I said. The backpack kept singing: all three tones, over and over. I zipped it open and started turning them off. "Lying down might be a good idea for all of us, actually." I clicked off the last doorbell ringer. "Everybody down, face on the floor, hands above your head."

"You can't save us," said Rain.

"Don't fight me on this," I said, but Harold reached over and turned off the lights. "Stop that—we need to be open and welcoming and harmless," I said. "Turning off the lights in this situation is deceptive and threatening."

"I can feel their minds," said Margo. "Your friend, too—Sam Harris. They know we're here but they don't know where. I'm going to—"

"No," I said again, as firmly as I could this time. "No mind control. You don't understand this: I'm going to save you, or at least I'm going to try very hard, but I can't do that if you take over even one of their minds. You have to be worth saving."

"I need to think," said Mr. Connor again.

"If you're going to be good, you have to be good," I said. "That's more than just not murdering anyone—it's no more manipulation, no more stripping people of their own free will. You can't be parasites anymore, you have to be equals."

"This is ridiculous," snarled Rain. "You think they're going to talk to us peacefully?"

"If we're peaceful first."

"You think we can just change who we are?"

"I did," I said. "My brain was broken, or is broken, and I don't know why or how or if it was my father or my mortuary or my DNA or what, but I want to kill people."

"What?" asked Jasmyn.

"I wanted to do it again tonight," I said, "when I had Agent Harris unconscious in the bathroom—I wanted to hurt him and crush him and cut him until you couldn't even tell who he was anymore, but I didn't. Because I don't let a broken brain tell me what to do. Because who you're supposed to be has nothing to do with who you actually are."

"They're getting closer," said Margo.

"I need to think," said Mr. Connor, and his voice was darker now, almost a growl of desperation. "I need to get out of this—I need to think!"

"Think about rules," I said. "I will not hurt people. Say it: I will not hurt people."

"I . . . don't know if I will or not!" growled Mr. Connor. "I need to think!"

"I will not hurt animals," I said. "I will not burn things. I will not call people 'it.'"

"The rules that worked for you aren't going to work for everybody," said Rain, "and even if they did, we can't just repeat a bunch of rules and magically become good people."

I nodded firmly. "Yes, you can, because I did. Say it: I will not hurt people."

"It doesn't work like this!" Rain shouted.

"You're going to come in here," said Mr. Connor. We heard the glass in the front door break, tiny shards clattering across the floor of the entryway. "Good," he said, "I need one."

"No you don't," I insisted. "You need self-control. It's not magic and it's not easy but it works." I looked at Rain. "And work is hard, and you'll struggle every day. But you can do it."

A sudden burst of gunfire echoed through the air, and I covered my head and ducked toward the ground, screaming that I needed more time. But then the shooting stopped abruptly, and we looked around, probing for damage in the darkness.

"Everyone okay?" asked Rain.

"Fine here," I said. I listened for movement in the hall but heard nothing.

"I think it was outside," said Jasmyn. We turned to the window, and she pulled aside the curtain. The sky was growing lighter—it was almost five in the morning and dawn was almost here. We saw cars, all black and unmarked, but only one person: a body, lying still and lifeless on the ground.

Soaking wet.

Shelley wailed.

"She's here," said Margo.

"Who's the drowner?" I asked. "The third Withered you were covering for—who is it? How does she work?"

"Her name is—" Margo started, but stopped suddenly when another man appeared out of nowhere, banging on the window and screaming in terror.

"Let me in!" he shouted. "Let me in! She's killing us! Let me in!"

Just as suddenly the man was caught in a storm—a rainstorm, or even a hurricane, so fierce and deadly it shattered the window and rattled the walls. Shards of glass flew in, and Jasmyn shrieked as the storm pelted her with water and glistening blades. I shielded my eyes, but then watched in horror as the falling water encircled the man, trapping him in wind and rain, cutting off all his air. His eyes bulged, his hands clawed uselessly at his rain-slick neck, and he suffocated completely, drowning barely three feet away from us. The fury of the storm abated, and the man fell dead to the ground.

"Her name is Dana," said Margo, and we watched as the tiny maelstrom shrank and shriveled and coalesced into a woman: the homeless woman. She looked at us with haunted eyes, and then her gaze locked onto me—not feral, like in the desert, but sharp and lucid and full of a fathomless sadness.

"I'll hold them off," said Dana. "Try to get away."

Then a bullet caught her shoulder and she exploded again, a warhead made of wind and water and fury, and she spun off across the front lawn toward the men who had attacked her.

"I made her sixty years ago," said Margo. "The first I'd tried since the old days. And the last."

"What did she give up?" I asked.

"Her mind," said Margo. "She has nothing in her head but chaos."

"Until she kills," I said, thinking about the tortured intelligence I'd seen in her face. "No mind at all until she steals one from a victim, and then she realizes what she's done."

"For sixty years," said Jasmyn.

"Try living like this for ten thousand," said Mr. Connor, "and then come crying to me about how hard it is." He froze, and then he looked up sharply. There was another crash of glass, and shouting and boots and the sudden, deafening roar of gunfire. The attack was inside this time.

Mr. Connor turned toward the door. "I need to think," he said, and ran into the hallway.

CHAPTER 19

Mr. Connor ran through the hall, with Harold close behind him; I sprinted to catch up, but they were too fast. We rounded a corner into the main hallway to find a group of three men in bulletproof vests—useless against the furious force of nature that had assailed them on the lawn—struggling to bar the shattered glass entrance with couches. Mr. Connor crouched low, but Harold roared and barreled forward in a rage.

"Stop!" I shouted, but he either didn't hear me or didn't care. The agents turned around just as Harold reached them, but they were holding a couch and couldn't defend themselves. Harold dropped one with a punch to the face, kicked another solidly in the stomach, and turned to grapple with the third.

"Rain!" I shouted; I turned to look for her, and she was close behind. "I told you not to hurt them!"

"I'm not," she said, and took cover in a doorway. "He's been controlled so long he just . . . It's instinct. He's not under my control right now, but he's not under his own, either. All he can do is defend me."

"Make him stop!"

"He's dead already," said Rain, and I turned back to see that it was true—the agents had recovered, dropping the couch in a broken heap and raising their weapons. Harold sunk his teeth into the shoulder of the man he was fighting, and when that man fell to the ground with a scream the other two men shot Harold a dozen times or more.

"No!" I shouted. "We have to stop!"

The agents turned toward us, and I saw Agent Harris standing in the middle of the group. They raised their guns, and Harris called out: "Nobody move!"

"I need a muse," Mr. Connor hissed, and raised up to run. I grabbed him, but he slapped at me with his hand—not slapped, but slashed, for his fingers had all elongated into eight-inch razors of yellowed bone. They raked my arm, as sharp as a surgeon's scalpels, and I fell backward as my skin opened up in four long lines. The cuts were deep, but so sharp I couldn't even feel them. Mr. Connor launched himself at the agents, and they fired back in an overwhelming volley; I dropped to the floor, covering my head with my hands and praying that none of the bullets flew wide enough to hurt me. The sound of the gunfire was deafening, drowning out even the screams. I think I screamed when something grabbed my legs, but it was lost in the noise, and no one could hear anything. I kept my hands tight over my head and felt myself get yanked help-lessly back into the darkness.

More hands grabbed me, pulling me farther; I slapped at them, but there were too many. When the shooting stopped I looked up, expecting the tooth-filled maw of a ravenous Withered, but I saw only Jasmyn, wide-eyed and panting, trying to sit me up against a wall. Rain was next to her.

"Are you okay?" I asked, but my ears were still ringing too loudly to hear my own voice, let alone her answer.

"They will never listen to us," said Rain, though it wasn't her voice but her mind, speaking directly to mine. Her thoughts entered mine like dragons in a medieval vil-lage, ancient and overwhelming, bringing destruction even where it wasn't intended; I felt memories and emo-tions and even reason corroding at her mental touch, top-pled as casually as a wooden hut caught by the flip of a great, forked tail.

"Let go of my mind," I shouted.

"Your hearing will return in a moment," said Ren, for now there was no other name for her but the primeval one—the mother of darkness. Her words rang through my mind like wailing spirits. "We need to get out of here."

"They'll only keep chasing us," I thought back. I felt like I was kneeling before an angry god. "We have to talk to them. Harris is there—let me reason with him."

"After all of this?" Her mental sneer scraped across my consciousness.

"They'll pin the mutilations on Mr. Connor," I thought, "and the Dark Lady stuff on Dana—they'll conflate that name with the drownings, just like I did. But they don't know about you. I'll save them later if I can, if I can find a way to reason with Harris, but we can save you now. Don't do anything suspicious or dangerous or supernatural and we can still get out of this."

"Jasmyn can," thought Ren. "And you. But not until after they cuff us and search us for weapons. At that point, there are certain things I can't hide. I'm too obviously Withered."

"So what will you do?" I asked.

Ren didn't answer, and I heard a distant shout. My hearing was coming back.

"I don't know," she thought at last. "I could fight back, and I could win."

"But you haven't yet," I said. That meant more than I dared to hope.

"No I haven't," she said at last.

"John!" I heard the voice, cutting through the ringing that still filled my physical ears. Ren pulled her thoughts away from mine, leaving me alone again in my own head, and the world seemed to snap back into focus. "John!" the voice shouted again. I took a deep breath, feeling a thousand pounds lighter than a moment ago. "John Cleaver, are you there?"

It was Harris's voice. I nodded, taking another breath, and then shouted back. "I'm here," I said. "I'm here. Are you okay?"

"Are you on their side?" he demanded.

I looked around and saw that Ren, Jasmyn, and I were holed up in the chapel, hiding behind a low wooden pew; the wide double door was riddled with bullets, and one side of it was hanging from a single hinge. Agent Harris's voice floated in from the hallway, probably still crouching in the shelter of their makeshift barricade.

"I'm trying to stop this fight," I said.

"Then you're on their side," he said. "They're the enemy, John, they need to be killed. There's no room for treaties here."

"Then the circle will never end," I said. "One side has to give."

"It's not going to be us," shouted Harris.

"That's okay," I said, "the other side already did. Now all you've got to do is stop shooting."

Harris's voice rose a few tones in disbelieving anger. "Are you kidding me? That thing you were with has already killed one of my men and dragged another off to who knows where—and that's not even counting what

Hurricane Katrina is doing to the rest of the team outside."

"She's trying to save us," I said. "It's complicated, but her heart's in right place."

"I can't wait to find out where Agent Gray's heart's going to be when that skinny guy gets through with him," snarled Harris. "Do you think he'll balance it on top of the guy's head, or maybe carve it open like a turnip rose first? Make a nice centerpiece or something."

"I tried to stop him!" I shouted. "And maybe all we can do is kill him, and if that's how it has to be then—"

"Maybe?" cried Harris. "John! He's killed three agents so far, and who knows how many more that we don't know about. He's been going for ten thousand years."

I closed my eyes. "People change."

"That'd be great if they did," said Harris, "but when? I have a responsibility to keep people safe, and I can't do that by letting a dangerous murderer go free. The circle can't end on him, John. That should be as clear to you as to anybody. And that thing outside can't end it, either, no matter how much you talk about her trying to do the right thing, because anyone who thinks that killing a dozen faithful law-enforcement officers counts as doing the right thing does not get to make any more of those decisions. They can't. And that third one . . ." he said, and I shook my head: he knew there was a third Withered. Ren shifted behind me, and I turned just in time to see her creep backward into the shadows. I clenched my jaw, trying to think of a way out of this. Everything was falling apart.

Harris continued his tirade: ". . . the third Withered, the mind controller, she tried to kill me once already. She tried to use me to kill my partner. She tried to kill you, John! For crying out loud, what does it take to piss you off anymore? Can't you see that these things are evil? That they need to be destroyed? I know you're trying to turn over a new leaf and be all good and righteous and I respect that; I applaud it. I think it's exactly the direction your life needs to go. But self-defense is a thing. You can't stalk someone and murder them for no reason, but when you see someone else doing it, it is your right—it is your responsibility—to step in and stop them. As an officer of the law or a citizen of it. And if that means killing the aggressor you do it, and that is right and legal and moral. The Withered are threatening the world and everybody in it merely by their existence; they kill and hurt and torture as a matter of course. It's as natural to them as breathing, and people like that cannot be allowed to live."

He stopped talking, though his words seemed to hang in the air like ghosts. I looked at Jasmyn, and she looked back. Terrified but determined. Ren was gone.

I looked back at the broken doorway. "Does that mean you would have killed me?"

He waited several seconds before answering: "That's different, John."

"No it's not."

"You're a human being!"

"So are they."

"They're killers!"

"So am I."

"You're a sociopath, John. You don't feel the difference between right and wrong, but you know it. You make choices to follow it, no matter how bad things get. They don't do that."

I smiled. "Then why aren't you being mind controlled right now?"

Agent Harris said nothing for a while. I crawled closer to Jasmyn, and she grabbed my hand and held it fiercely.

"Is she here?" asked Harris.

"She is," I said. "I don't know where, but she's definitely close enough to hurt you if she wanted to. But she's not."

"Then she's planning something," said Harris. "This whole building is a trap."

"Occam's razor," I said. "Why use an elaborate trap when she could just make you all shoot yourselves in a couple of seconds?"

He paused again, then shouted back: "Are you armed?"

"No."

"Then why are we shouting?"

"Because you don't believe me," I said.

A moment later Harris peeked his head around the edge of the blasted door. I stood up and pulled Jasmyn with me. Harris stepped inside and pointed his gun at us.

"Jasmyn Shahi?"

"I'm not armed either," she said, and I saw that she kept her cool well enough not to raise her arms at the sight of his gun. "And I'm not a Withered or whatever the hell."

"Hell is close enough," said Harris. Now that he was close I could see a bad cut on the side of his head, and a patch of purple skin and dried blood around it. "I'm going to pat you both down just to be sure."

"Oh, my word," I said.

"I'm not an idiot, John."

"I just gave you a whole speech about breaking the cycle of violence," I said, though I let go of Jasmyn's hand and spread my arms and legs wide. "I'm not hiding a shower curtain in my back pocket, if that's what you're worried about."

He patted my legs and chest with a sneer. "I bet you've been saving that one all friggin' night, haven't you?"

"The woman we're looking for is named Ren," I said.

"The demon queen?" He satisfied himself that I was not armed and moved on to Jasmyn. She didn't look remotely comfortable letting a man touch her, but she bit her tongue and stared at the wall. I let Harris finish before I started talking again; Jasmyn jogged several steps away the instant she was allowed to.

"Ren doesn't want to hurt anyone," I said. "But there's only three of them left and they feel kind of backed against a wall. Understandably, I think."

Harris looked up as we heard more shouts and shooting in the distance. "I think our feelings are pretty damn understandable as well."

"Everyone's feeling are," I said. "That's what makes this so hard."

"I don't hear any more shooting," said Jasmyn. "Or screaming."

I nodded. "You think Dana's gone?"

"Is that the hurricane girl?" asked Harris.

"Yeah."

"She's gone," he said, "or she's come inside."

"Then we need to find Mr. Connor," said Jasmyn. "We might still be able to save the agent he took."

Harris sucked in a breath, considering his options and obviously hating them all. "Yeah," he said at last, "you're probably right."

"You're way too optimistic," I said, "but you're right anyway." I started walking toward the door. "Mr. Connor's building another muse; he needs them for anything deeper than computational thought."

"What about Ren?" asked Harris. "I don't want to leave a demon queen unaccounted for."

"If she was attacking us we'd know," I said, and I caught just the hint of an involuntary shudder that ran through Harris's head and shoulders as I said it. He'd felt that same horrible thing I had. But Ren still wasn't attacking.

We went into the hall, and Jasmyn picked up the rifle

from the fallen FBI agent. Harris raised his eyebrow. "You know how to use that?"

"This is small-town America," said Jasmyn. "Half the dates I've been on have been to a gun range."

"Fair enough," said Harris.

"Did you see which way he went?" I asked.

"This hallway," said Harris, pointing toward the embalming room. We followed the hall cautiously, listening for sounds, but heard nothing. I checked in the embalming room; there were wet footprints on the tile, but no people or bodies.

"What else is down this hallway?" asked Harris.

"The crematorium," said Jasmyn.

"Awesome," Harris said, and shuddered again.

We crept softly down the hall, poking our heads into each room as we passed it—the restroom, the coatroom, a custodial closet—but Mr. Connor wasn't in any of them. I looked for wet footprints in the carpet but couldn't see any. No shouts or cries rang out in the distance; no bodies lay bleeding or soaking on the floor. We were alone in the house of the dead. With three Withered demons.

We approached the crematorium slowly, the last room at the end of the hall. The door hung open, and we could see now the faint hint of red and the subtle roar of flame. Someone had turned it on. I waved Harris and Jasmyn back a few steps, and peeked into the room as quietly as I could.

Blood covered the floor and walls, and a totem made of human flesh rose from the center of the floor.

Agent Gray's body had been disassembled and the pieces had been carefully stacked and balanced in a grotesque new configuration. The torso, headless and limbless, sat at the base, with a careful arrangement of handless arms and footless legs forming an intricate web of arches and buttresses above it. Within this web was the head, too concealed to see clearly, and sprouting from it were hands and fingers and feet and toes, spraying out from the edges like leaves and spikes and horns. I couldn't tell how they were attached. On one side of the room the oven burned fiercely, bathing the room in a hellish orange glow, and next to it, cross-legged on the ground, sat Mr. Connor, his fingers steepled solemnly in front of his face. Directly across from him, in the dancing light of the fire, the corpse-made monument cast a writhing, rippling shadow against the wall.

Mr. Connor watched that shadow and dreamed.

"Don't come in unless you really want to see this," I said, and then stepped further into the room. Agent Harris followed, his face grim and flat. A moment later, hesitant and wary, Jasmyn came in as well. She balked when she saw the display, but didn't back out. Death was her life now, and corpses had become so clinical they couldn't faze her. Even this one.

"What do you see?" asked Mr. Connor.

I looked at the body, at the muse he had so carefully

constructed, and once again I had the unnerving thought that it *meant* something, that it was saying something in a language that my head or my heart or my soul could speak, even if I, myself, couldn't remember a word of it. It was a hieroglyph, or a pictogram, or something even more primitive; it was a trail marker, flat stones stacked up to show where one hunter had passed before, so that another could follow behind. Slashes cut into a tree. I looked at my own arm, sliced with four neat lines by one killer, and raked with a chaos of scratches by another. Ancient carvings, to mark the path.

"It's not true," I said.

Mr. Connor stared at the shadows. "Nothing is."

"It's marking a path," I said, "but the path isn't true— it isn't the right path just because it's marked. We don't have to follow it."

Mr. Connor's voice was low, like a drumbeat in the distance. "There's only one path now. The only path we've ever had." He rose to his feet, fluid and almost majestic in the firelight. "This is why I need the muse—to tell me what I see."

"What do you see?" asked Jasmyn.

"Dancing shadows," said Mr. Connor. "Real and unreal at once."

"Like the Withered," said Harris.

"Like everything," said Mr. Connor, and then the bones slid out from his fingertips, as thin and precise as a sculptor's tools. "I grew up in a cave, you know. Before the ritual, when I was still a child. It doesn't mean anything, but this made me think of it."

"We can get out of this," I said, watching his claws warily, putting myself between him and the others. "We can make this right."

"The only way out is down," he said, and then he leapt toward me with a hiss. Harris and Jasmyn both fired their weapons, deafening me again, but the bullets simply punched through him and sparked against the cement wall behind, and Mr. Connor slashed at me with his blades. I tumbled backwards, falling to the ground, and Mr. Connor descended toward me with a soundless howl, but he never landed. A burst of wind filled the room, catching him up and surrounding him with a torrent of air and water. Dana had come. She held him in the air, invisible and intangible and impervious to his flailing claws, and then the water condensed out of the air and covered his head. He fought and slashed and kicked and screamed, but no sound came out; he clawed at his own throat, desperate for air, but the only thing constricting it was water, and all he did was slash his own face, his own skin, his own neck and throat and sinew. Water and blood leaked out only to flow back in, forced through him by the wind, and then his struggles grew weaker and his arms fell and then he stopped altogether. And then it wasn't blood leaking from his wounds but soulstuff—ash and grease and tar, as black as the darkest shadow. He crumbled before our eyes, shriveling in on himself at the heart of the raging storm. And when the storm suddenly abated, it wasn't a body that fell, but a slick, runny blob. It splashed against the floor, spattering us with sludge both warm and cold at once.

Mr. Connor was dead.

CHAPTER 20

Dana appeared in the room, condensing like dew from the moisture in the air. Her bare feet touched down lightly on the floor, and she watched us with eyes sunk deep into her skull. Her hair hung tangled and stringy in a frame around her face.

We looked back, too frightened to speak.

"Is it safe to assume," said Harris at last, "that if you wanted us dead we'd already be dead?"

"You're safe for now," said Dana. Her tattered dress dripped tiny drops of water on the floor, splashing and mixing with the sludge from Mr. Connor's death. The muse, toppled by the storm, sat in meaningless, powerless heaps upon the floor.

"So, what can we do," asked Jasmyn, "to make sure that doesn't change?"

"Nothing," said Dana. "Stay away from me, I guess."

"Is that a threat?" asked Harris.

"It's a weather report," said Dana, and sighed. "No pun intended."

"She won't be lucid forever," I said, watching her carefully. "Maybe longer than normal, after so many victims, but it'll fade eventually."

"Her mind?" asked Harris.

"Her control," I said, and took a step toward her. "How long does it last, usually?"

"There's no way to predict it," she said. "Part of the deal, I suppose. Part of the chaos. I didn't want rules; I didn't want to feel trapped in somebody else's way of thinking. I wanted to be free, I guess, and now I'm free of everything." She breathed in and tried to smile, and the feigned good humor was more painful to look at than the sadness. "My mind's so open I can't hold anything in it."

"Then Mr. Connor was right," said Harris. "The only way out is down." He looked at me, so tired and frustrated and broken he was practically laughing. "Don't you get it, John? We have to keep fighting them because they have to keep fighting us. It's never stopped for ten thousand years, and it's not going to stop now just because we want it to."

"I came to the same conclusion," said Ren, and we spun around, guns raised, to see her standing in the doorway. Agent Harris maneuvered himself closer to the wall, where he could see both women at once, and moved his eyes and gun back and forth between them, twitchy and terrified.

"Either one of them could kill us in a second if they wanted," I told him, "but they don't. So just stay calm."

"She just said she's planning to fight," said Harris.

"I didn't say it to you," said Ren, and her voice held the authority of ten thousand years. "John's the one who deserves an explanation—you keep quiet and try not to attract my attention."

"Maybe Dana can't control herself," I said to Ren, "but you can. You're smart, you're powerful, you're an ancient goddess, for crying out loud."

"That's exactly why I can't follow your rules," said Ren. "I have to be me—I can't let other people make all my choices for me."

"So, you choose to kill?" I said. "You choose to fight and hurt and maim and destroy?"

"I choose to live the way I want to live," said Ren. "That's never been any more violent than anybody else, but the world still wants to kill me for it."

"I can think of three people you tried to kill in the last six hours alone," said Harris.

"I was trying to help," said Ren fiercely, but then her voice softened, and she looked at her palms. "It just . . . got out of hand."

"So, you fight and you die," said Jasmyn. "John and Harris and I here, presumably, and then you later on, and what does that get us?"

"It gets us freedom," said Ren. "And when we finally die, at least we die making our own choices, under our own control."

"You're not under your own control," said Dana. "And you're not free."

"I'm the mother of darkness," said Ren. "Who do you think is controlling me?"

"Pride," said Dana. "Selfishness."

"I've heard the church-and-sin talk plenty of times before," said Ren. "You can save it for next time you give someone a speech."

"You don't want to be controlled?" asked Dana. "I gave up my control when I did your ritual, and I lived my life without anyone telling me what to do. And it wasn't a life worth living." She started walking as she spoke, tracing a small arc across the floor of the room; Harris tracked her with his gun. "Choosing to follow rules isn't giving up control," she said, "it's controlling yourself. That doesn't seem like a superpower, but try it for sixty years and tell me what you think about it then." She stopped in front of the oven, and her shadow fell across the room like a storm cloud. "I've killed five people this morning, one of them a Withered." She stared into the flames as she spoke. "Ten thousand years old. I have more control now than I've ever had before."

"What are you going to with it?" asked Harris. I didn't say a word, because I already knew.

"Honey," said Ren, "don't you dare do what I think you're going to do."

"I'm going to do what you won't do," said Dana, holding a hand to the heat of the flames. "I'm going to break the cycle. You can't stop me from killing, Agent Harris, but I can stop myself."

"No!" shouted Ren, but Dana seemed to explode into a storm again, a furious maelstrom of wind and water and chaos—but now, for one brief window of time, controlled by a powerful presence of mind. Her storm surged into the oven, hissing and steaming as the water expanded, but the intelligence behind it kept pulling back in, reining in the clouds and forcing them over and over into the heat of the flames. Steam hit the ceiling and condensed into big, heavy drops, only to come back into the fire again, over and over, endless and relentless, until the cloud grew smaller and the steam grew darker, and the harsh, acrid smell of tar filled the room like a toxic mist. I walked to the side of the oven and turned it off, and the flames disappeared. The inside of the oven was coated with soulstuff, brittle and burned into charcoal.

Ren was crying.

Agent Harris turned his gun on her.

"Don't do it," I said.

"Last one left," said Harris. "I can end it here."

"Don't end it by killing," I pleaded, and looked at Ren. "End it by choosing."

"I don't want to burn myself," said Ren.

"You don't have to," I said. "You just have to promise. Don't hurt anyone—don't destroy any lives, don't control any minds. I know that's all in your nature, but you can be better than that." I stopped talking and stared at her, trying to make her understand. "Ren," I said, and then, after a pause, "Margo."

She looked up.

"I'm the worst person I know," I said. "If I can do it, anyone can."

"That can't possibly be true," said Margo. "Most of the people you know are monsters."

"Everyone's worth saving," I said. "Even monsters."

Margo looked at me, and I looked at her, and I thought about what I was doing. Did I really know? Was I really certain she could change? Was any of this really worth it? I looked at her, and I thought about my mother.

And I knew.

"Let me stay with her," I said. "Tell the FBI that we're dead, and that the war's over, and leave us here. You can drop in every now and then if you want, but I'll stay here, and I'll help her stay clean."

"I can't have a family," said Margo. "It's part of the pact—I gave that up. I can't have children, and I can't be needed."

"I can be," I said simply. "Maybe that'll be enough."

We watched each other, and Harris watched us, his eyes flicking back and forth from Margo to me to Margo.

"It's not that easy," he said. "For all the reasons I told you before. The government wants you locked in a cell that nobody even knows exists."

"But you know me better than they do," I said. "Death follows me because I've been hunting Withered, but if I'm not then it won't. I'll stay here—you know I will." I looked at him. "You're a criminal profiler, and I'm practically your entire career. As depressing as this sounds, you know me better than anyone in the world."

He stared at me and then shook his head—not in argument, but in disbelief.

"You'd be under constant, omnipresent surveillance," said Harris. "And you, personally, would be responsible for everything. If I have to come back here next week or month or whatever for some kind of mind-controlled, arsonist, crazy-ass murder spree, I'm going to be very disappointed. And that disappointment will be measured in platoons of active-duty soldiers, adequately equipped to kill Godzilla."

"We'll be fine," said Jasmyn.

"You're not a part of this arrangement," said Harris.

"My best friends are a serial killer and the Mother of Darkness," said Jasmyn. "Try to stop me."

Harris rolled his eyes but holstered his pistol. "Fine. But give me that gun back. And be prepared for a very long interview process before this is all over. Five FBI agents died on this property today, and even if I can manage to fake your death, John, this isn't going to go away easy."

"I believe in you," I said. "Super-Best-Friends Powers, activate!"

"Shut up."

CHAPTER 21

"Say it with me," I said. " 'Today I will think good thoughts and smile at everyone I see.' "

Margo stared at me across her desk. "You know I hate this."

"More than government execution?" I asked. "Because that's a lot of hatred."

"It's getting up there," said Margo, and she grimaced. "Maybe it's time for another pressure valve. What's it been, five months? Six?"

"Five months, three weeks, and two days," I said. I adjusted my new hearing aid—too many gunshots in an enclosed space do some pretty permanent damage. "One hundred and sixty-eight days with neither a workplace injury nor a rage-fueled binge of pent-up supernatural terrorism."

"You make that sound like a long time," said Margo.

"You want a button?" I asked. "Alcoholics Anonymous gives you a button when you hit a milestone—"

"Don't get smart with me."

"I can't help it."

"'Helping it' is the entire point of this conversation," said Margo. "Show some self-control before I give you extra mopping duty or something."

I smiled, and she looked at the calendar on her desk.

"Has been a while since the last pressure valve, though," she said. "Think it's time?"

"Mine or yours?" I asked. Our "pressure valves" were activities that helped us stay in control of the important stuff by letting loose a little on the small stuff. For her it usually meant volunteering for something—she got to boss people around without the use of mind control, and she got to form relationships. For me, we usually just went out in the desert and lit something on fire.

Very big somethings. It was awesome.

"Yours," said Margo. "I think I can go another week or so."

"Same," I said, and smiled. "You still haven't said it with me."

"Said what?"

"You know what."

She gave an exasperated sigh. "Dammit, John, I have important things to do!"

"Not as important as this."

"Fine," she said, and we recited it together: "Today I will think good thoughts, and smile at everyone I see."

"Are you happy now?" she said.

"As a sociopath I'm technically never happy—"

"You are the snottiest little—"

"I'm happy," I said, "I'm happy. You still got your rules on your mirror at home?"

"And I read them every day," she said, and laughed. "Someone's going to have some awfully difficult questions if they ever use my bathroom and wonder why I have a sign taped up that says 'I will ask for what I want instead of controlling people's minds.'"

"Just tell them the truth," I said. "With lives like ours, no one believes it anyway."

She chuckled softly, tapping her finger on the desk, but then she sighed, and the corners of her mouth turned down.

"This can't last forever," she whispered.

"Nothing does."

"You're going to leave."

"Never."

"Then you're going to die," she said. "Even if it's not for a hundred more years—do you think I haven't had friendships before? Do you think I haven't built relation-ships with people, just to watch them grow old and die while I just continued on? Even if you think you know how long ten thousand years is, I guarantee that you do not."

"I haven't lost as many people as you have," I said, "but the ones I've lost were . . . significant. And it hurts, and I'm sorry."

"You think you're ever going to see them again?"

"Brooke, maybe," I said. "Someday. Probably better for her if I don't."

"She loves you."

"All the more reason to stay away."

Margo smiled slyly. "When are you going to ask Jasmyn out?"

"Why does everyone keep asking that?"

"Because you'd be stupid not to."

"She's not my type," I said.

"Alive?"

"That was low," I said, pointing at her. "You don't see me in here . . . pushing all your psychological buttons—"

My backpack sang out: *ding-dong, ding-dong.*

Margo raised her eyebrow. "You turned those things back on again?"

"It's been almost six months," I said, standing up. "Agent Harris is going to check in on us any day now."

"Did he give you a schedule?"

"No," I said, peeking out of the curtain. "I just know him. And there's your car, you little FBI twerp. I know you as well as you know m—"

And then I heard a dog bark, and I froze in place.

"John?" asked Margo.

"Can you . . ." I peered out the window, but I couldn't see anyone. "Can you tell a dog by its bark?"

"I guess so," she said. "Depends on how well you know the dog."

"I could swear I know this one," I said, and moved out into the hall. Margo stood up and followed.

Agent Harris opened the front door, and Boy Dog waddled in. He sniffed the air and barked again, and I stopped. Boy Dog looked around, snuffling his nose against the floor, checking out the entryway to make sure it wasn't filled with bacon, and then trundled over to me and sat down, his warm, fat bulk resting just on the edge of my toes.

"Hey John," said Harris. "Brought you something."

"Thanks," I said. I stared at Boy Dog, half convinced he wasn't even real. But he was.

"Is this that dog you keep talking about?" asked Jasmyn, stepping out of the chapel. "Lean down and pet him, for goodness sake, what kind of joyful reunion is this?"

"Trust me," said Harris, watching my face. "This is about as joyful as I've ever seen him." He winked. "At least so far."

I raised my eyebrow. "Do I get a pony, too?"

"The United States government docs not trust you with a pony at this time," said Harris. "But yeah, I've got someone else here to see you."

"Not Brooke," I said, and took a step backward. Boy Dog whined at the shift in his bulk. "I can't see her. I'm not ready to see her."

Margo gripped my shoulders tightly. "It's okay," she said. "Whatever it is, we're going to be okay."

Harris looked to the door and nodded, and then beckoned again with his hand. Someone outside reached for the handle and pushed it open and stepped inside, and I thought for just one brief, tiny moment that it was my mother.

"Aunt Margaret," I whispered, and then another woman came in behind her. "Lauren."

"Oh my gosh," said Lauren when she saw me, and her eyes filled with tears. "You're so tall!"

"Hey," I said, and then because I couldn't think of anything else: "Do you . . ." I swallowed. ". . . know?"

"Yeah," said Lauren.

"Everything?"

"Yeah," said Lauren, nodding, and she glanced at Margo. "Everything."

"And you're . . . okay?"

She laughed, wiping the tears from her eyes. "John, we love you. No matter what."

"Hey John," said Margaret. "You look . . . Do you mind if . . ." Her eyes were wet, and she put her hand over her mouth. She tried again. "John, can I give you a hug?"

"Sure," I said, and she opened her arms, and I walked

up and hugged her, and Lauren hugged us both, and we were all crying and swaying and holding each other more tightly than I'd ever held anybody ever before.

And I was happy.